Inside

Inside

Dan Morgan

A BERKLEY MEDALLION BOOK
PUBLISHED BY
BERKLEY PUBLISHING CORPORATION

BERKLEY MEDALLION BOOKS are published by
Berkley Publishing Corporation
200 Madison Avenue
New York, N.Y. 10016

BERKLEY MEDALLION BOOKS ® TM 757,375

Printed in the United States of America

Berkley Medallion Edition, DECEMBER, 1974

CHAPTER ONE

There were five dead people in the shelter afterwards. Four of them stood facing Gerry Clyne, their clothes caked with soot and filth, the embers of panic dying slowly in their eyes. He looked at them, deliberately closing his mind to unbidden, insistent thoughts of the fifth. Later those thoughts would have to be admitted, but now, with the acrid stench of smoke still fouling his nostrils, it was time to think of survival.

Working together, they had managed to put the fire out at last, but it was a hollow victory. The food which was to have sustained them for twelve months had been destroyed, the living quarters were completely gutted, and the upper level, in which they now stood, had only been preserved at the cost of all but a few gallons of the precious supply of uncontaminated water.

These four living dead still had a certain choice in the manner of their death. They could remain where they were until they eventually perished from starvation and thirst—or they could go outside. Out there their bodies would absorb a killing dose of radioactivity in something less than ten minutes, but the dying would take longer, a great deal longer. With the protection of antiradiation suits they might have been able to survive long enough to find another sanctuary, but so far none of them seemed to have realized that those suits now lay beneath the smouldering wreckage of the main storeroom. Instead they stood, looking to him through force of habit as their natural leader, expecting that he would produce some miraculous solution.

Now that the insulating effect of adrenalin was fading from his bloodstream, the burns on his arms and face were becoming more painful every second. He might have saved himself that pain, for all the good done by his dash through the flames to Kay's room, but he knew that he would never have been able to forgive himself if he had failed to make at least some attempt to save the woman who had brought a new awareness

1

of the dimensions of love into his life. Added to this was the memory that it had been himself who had, earlier that night, administered the drug injection which had released her from the choking terror of yet another asthmatic/claustrophobic attack—the same drug which was to bind her comatose as the pitiless flames ravaged her body.

By the time Palance had awakened him it was already too late. If they had thought about her at all in their panic after the discovery of the fire, the others had assumed that she was with him, safe in his private quarters on the upper level. By the time he arrived at her room it was already an inferno, and she . . . His mind shied away from the memory of the horror he had found. That twisted, charred thing was no longer Kay. He had turned and left the flames to complete their now merciful task of disintegration.

There was little satisfaction in laying the blame for her death on Palance and Mitchell. Clearly the fire would not have got such a hold before it was detected if they had been doing their jobs, but they would pay the price for that neglect with their lives.

Not he. With or without Kay, there was no uncertainty in his mind about the fact that he must go on living. The others only existed now as a fringe benefit of his own foresight. Without his protection they would have died a month ago, along with the other 99 percent of the population.

The shelter had cost Gerry Clyne several millions, but he had not quibbled about the price. Money and power were no use without life, and the shelter was necessary for survival. It had been designed by Garfield Burton, the best architect he could buy; an immensely strong shell of concrete and steel, embedded beneath the sandstone mass of the hill, a perfect life-support system, capable of protecting its occupants against any catastrophes, natural or man-made. When the hellish rain of ICBMs began to fall it had fulfilled the purpose for which it had been intended, protecting Clyne and his companions against blast, heat and radiation—*from the outside*.

Inside, perhaps because of his very confidence in the impregnability of the outer structure, or through some perverse blind spot, Burton's judgement had been less sound.

2

Apart from the provision of two small carbon tetrachloride extinguishers, one for each level of the shelter, he seemed to have overlooked the possibility of an internally generated fire in his calculations. The extinguishers had proved almost useless as the flames roared through the highly inflammable plastic and wood of the lower level apartments, and in the confined space the toxic fumes produced by their use had constituted an added hazard.

But there was no point now in thinking of Burton, who had probably been killed in those first few terrible hours of the missile war. On the surface in the area of the shelter there had been no sign of life for over two weeks now, and it was nearly three since the remote-controlled machine guns that guarded the entrance had been activated by anyone passing through the constantly watching beams. The only people surviving now could be those who had been able to retreat into deep shelters and, barring the unlikely possibility of a direct hit, those who had been inside Dome City before the beginning of the holocaust.

"What do we do now, G.C.?" Buzz Mitchell broke the silence. A month ago he had been a snappy dresser, alert, respectful in an unservile manner, one of the best bodyguards in the business. Now, wearing only a pair of greasy light-weight slacks and a soiled tee shirt, a growing paunch spilling over his belt, he was an unwashed, surly slob.

Elbert Inman, still wearing his carefully immaculate jacket, collar and tie, rimless octagonal glasses in place on his pale, thin nose, stood with one protective arm round Clare Inman's bony shoulders. "I fail to see any reason for undue alarm," he said, his voice even now carrying the prim self-assurance of his professional image. "We shall be needing more food and water, of course. But with the main power supply still functioning, I fail to see any reason why we should not hold out here indefinitely."

I fail to see . . . Gerry mused ironically on the blinkered pomposity of the repeated phrase. It was typical of Inman, devout supporter of the local Chamber of Commerce, pillar of the church and ostentatious social do-gooder, to sound such a note of sweet reasonableness. Inman and his raddled, horse-toothed wife, who had fallen over themselves to accept

3

the offer of sanctuary, despite their covert disapproval of himself, his unashamed enjoyment of his self-made wealth, and his relationship with Kay, whose first husband had been one of their own bloodless in-group. Gerry had not made the offer out of any desire for their company, they were far from his idea of a fun couple, but their home was nearby, and it had seemed possible that Inman's medical skills might prove useful.

"You think the supermarket will still be open, Doc?" Palance stood slightly removed from the other three, his contemptuous dark eyes on Inman. Inman, for all his pomposity, was unimportant in this situation, and Buzz Mitchell's mind was dulled by inaction and constant dosage from the store of alcohol he had managed to smuggle into the shelter. Neither of them could possibly represent any serious threat to the execution of Gerry's survival plan. Palance was another matter; a deadly, gutterbred killer, with slim, Latin good looks, his intelligence and ruthlessness had made him useful in the past, but might now represent a certain danger.

Inman's thin lips tightened. "Obviously there must be considerable supplies of undamaged canned goods and dried foods in the area."

"A nice mess of radioactive beans?" jibed Palance.

"We have radiation counters," Inman said. "It should be quite a simple matter to tell which foods have remained free from contamination. And as far as water is concerned, there must be a number of underground storage tanks in the area."

"Sounds fine, Doc. I just hope it's going to be that easy." Palance turned his head and looked directly at Clyne. "What do you think, G.C.?"

Gerry returned the stare of the hard, dark eyes, and found himself wondering just how much Palance knew, or had guessed. Certainly he would have preferred to avoid the direction in which the conversation was moving at the present time.

"We shall be able to make a much better assessment of the situation tomorrow," he said. "As soon as it's daylight, I'll take a look around the immediate area. In the meantime, I think it would be a good idea if we all tried to get some sleep." He turned to Mitchell. "Buzz, there should be some

4

spare blankets and stuff in the emergency store for those who want them. Go and check, will you?''

''You're suggesting that we should all sleep in here?'' Inman said, glancing round the open expanse of the control room.

''It's either that, or the generator room, and I don't think anybody would get much rest in there,'' said Clyne. ''Later on it may be possible to clean up part of the lower level.''

''I don't mind for myself, you understand,'' Inman said. ''But after all, Clare . . . Do you think perhaps she might use your room temporarily?''

''No—I don't,'' Gerry said, flatly.

Palance deliberately placed a different interpretation on the suggestion. ''I didn't know you had Eskimo blood, Doc,'' he said, grinning. ''But if that's the way you feel about it, don't forget that I'm a twenty-eight day virgin.''

One corner of Inman's thin mouth twitched as he flashed a look of sheer hatred at Palance. Tightening his grip on his wife's scrawny shoulder, he led her away across to the other side of the room, as the bodyguard grinned in appreciation of his own crude humor.

Gerry realized that this was only the beginning. Palance would start carefully pushing harder and harder to see just how far he could go, assessing the situation move by move until he finally made his bid for control. But before that time came . . . ''Go check on what Buzz is doing, will you?'' Gerry said. He turned abruptly and walked towards the door of his own quarters.

His accommodation was very little different from that of the now destroyed apartments on the lower level. The walls were finished in pale cream eggshell paint, and there were the same self-contained shower and toilet facilities. The main difference was in the size of the bed-sitting room, which had been made larger in order to accommodate a desk and chair, and the big gray metal locker that stood in one corner.

He stripped down and showered, wasting several more gallons of precious water with a prodigality that would have shocked Inman. Using the towel carefully, he dried himself off and dabbed soothing ointment onto his burns. By the time he had put on clean trousers and a short sleeved shirt he was feeling considerably better and wide awake. Now that Kay was dead there could be no doubt about his next move. There was a growing impatience in him to begin, but he reminded himself that it would be dawn in only three hours and the journey would be less hazardous in daylight. He lay on top of the bed and willed himself to relax.

He had been lying there for about half an hour when he heard the sound, tiny but unmistakable. He lifted himself on one elbow and watched the door handle moving slowly downwards.

"Come in, Palance," he said quietly.

Palance closed the door behind him. In his right hand he was holding a small automatic, a woman's weapon, but easily concealed and deadly. The muzzle pointed steadily at Gerry. "You were expecting me?"

"Who else," Gerry said, evenly. "Are the rest of them asleep?"

Palance nodded. "Yes. Now perhaps you and me can talk some sense, real sense about what happens next."

"Sure, why not?" Gerry said. He pointed at the gun. "But you don't need that thing to talk."

"Let's call it a safety precaution." Palance leaned with his back against the door, apparently perfectly at ease. But Gerry had seen the man in action too many times to believe that the pose indicated relaxation. Unlike Mitchell, Palance had not allowed his time in the shelter to soften the keen edge of his professional alertness. He was still a ruthless killing machine, capable of bursting into destructive action at any second, and Gerry knew that he would have to act carefully if he was not to trip that hair-trigger violence.

"All right, if it makes you feel better," he said. "So what are your views on what happens next?"

Palance's cruel mouth twisted in a grin. "You know what they say about you, G.C.? They say if you fell in a cess-pit you'd come up smelling of roses, and with a new idea in aftershaves that would make you a million."

"Improbable, but I get the implication. So. . . ?"

"I've watched you operate for nearly three years now," Palance said, "long enough to understand that gags like that are only part of the story. Main thing is that you're not one of those people things just happen to.''

"Captain of my fate and master of my soul?" Gerry grinned easily. "We're none of us exactly that."

"Maybe not, but you know what I mean," Palance said. "I've never yet seen you at a loss, when you didn't already have your next move figured in detail."

"Perhaps that's just how it looked to you. Sometimes I'm just following my nose and hoping."

"All right, so you think on your feet and adapt as you go along, but you don't miss any angles."

Slowly and carefully, constantly aware of the menace of the gun, Gerry lowered his legs over the edge of the bed and moved to a sitting position.

"You seem to have made quite a study of me, Palance. So I don't miss any angles. What's that got to do with the present situation?"

"Quite a bit, I think," Palance said. "Like for instance the fact you were very careful not to mention earlier—that if anybody is going to get out of here and go shopping for food and water, he's going to need an antiradiation suit."

"I should have thought that was too obvious to need mentioning."

"Except that we both know the antiradiation suits were kept down in the main storeroom on the lower level, which means that even if we could find them in all that junk it's a hundred-to-one against their being any use."

"You really have been thinking, haven't you, Palance? And have you come up with a solution?"

"Could be. Like I said—you're not the kind of person things just happen to—you've always got some sort of alternative plan."

"I could hardly have taken the fire into my considerations."

"Maybe not," Palance said. "But you must have had some escape route in mind, just in case the shelter didn't come up to expectations."

"Escape route—to where? You know as well as I do that there just isn't anywhere to go. There are other shelters in the area—old Van Der Groot over on Hillcrest had one built twice this size, but he's not taking in guests, that's for sure. His guards would blow your head off before you got within a quarter of a mile of the place.''

"Like we did with those poor, ragged bastards three weeks ago?'' Palance said. "Ironic isn't it? The whole damned world gone to hell, and all you can do is dig a hole and defend it against all comers, like a grizzly.''

"Or a rat. That's the way the world is—the way it's always been. You know that, Palance.''

"All right, so you intended to go further. I figured that much already. Maybe as far as Dome City? With forty or so square miles they'd have room for a few extra in there, wouldn't they?''

So Palance knew about Dome City. Gerry met the steady, reptilian gaze of the dark eyes, aware that his life depended on his successful handling of the next few minutes. "They might,'' he said, "always provided they didn't cop a direct hit when all that atomic hardware was flying around.''

"I don't think that's likely—neither do you. A couple of hundred miles from anywhere, and on nobody's maps. . . .''

"You must be joking,'' Gerry said. "The other side have got satellites up there that can read the small print on a dollar bill. You think they wouldn't know about the existence of a geodesic dome covering an area that size?''

"Not if it was surrounded by a battery of tri-diprojectors that made it look just like another hunk of desert, projectors that were set up long before any building was begun, a perfect camouflage. Let's not try to fool each other, G.C.—we both know that Monarch Engineering, your own firm, had a contract worth a hundred million to handle part of the construction.''

"You're very well informed, for a . . .''

"A hired thug?'' Palance grinned. "Don't mix me up with Mitchell, G.C. I carry most of my muscle in my head, if you see what I mean. I make it my business to know things, to notice what's going on around me. For instance, one of the last things you did before coming in here, even though time was getting short, and the first ICBM couldn't have been more than a couple of minutes away, was to check on that

8

two-seater sports flyer you've got stowed away in the rein-forced bunker on the other side of the hill. My guess is that you never did intend to stay down here any longer than you were absolutely forced. This was just a temporary bolt-hole, until the bombs stopped dropping and the worst of the radiation was over.''

''What makes you say that?'' Gerry asked, genuinely curious.

''Because down here, with only five other people, is too small a kingdom for a man like you, G.C. Simple survival might be enough for the time being, but you knew that it wouldn't be long before the old power bug was goosing you along and you were chafing for something to organize, to take over.''

''And then?''

''Obvious—you planned to get out of here and head for Dome City, the only place left on the whole damned continent—perhaps in the world—with sufficient people and resources to occupy your talents. The way I see it, the fire hasn't made a lot of difference to your plans, except that now you'll be making your move sooner, rather than later.''

''Interesting,'' Gerry said. ''But haven't you forgotten the point you were talking about earlier? Without an antiradia-tion suit, nobody is going to go anywhere out there and live.''

''No, G.C. I haven't forgotten that, and neither did you. There were four suits down there in the main store. I saw them myself only a couple of days ago. *Four* . . . but you didn't give a damn when you knew they'd been destroyed.''

''How can you be sure of that? Perhaps I just didn't want to panic the others.''

''And perhaps you're just planning on sitting around here and waiting to die?'' Palance laughed harshly. ''No, G.C.—not *you*. You don't give up that easily. You had your escape route organized, and the fire didn't make any differ-ence, did it?''

Didn't make any difference, thought Gerry. *God! how little you know*. But then such a situation would be com-pletely outside of Palance's experience—as it had been out of his own until Kay came along and changed his life. There had been women, many of them forgotten now, others remem-

9

bered through some shadowy memory, but none with whom he had shared a relationship as he had with Kay. Always before, because of some lack in them, or in himself, part of him had remained detached, uninvolved. Only with Kay had he experienced the loss of self-preoccupation, the sharing that made the act of loving something more than a passing sensual pleasure. And now Kay was dead. And because she was dead. . . .

"Four suits, but six people. You wouldn't miss out on a detail like that, G.C.—not you," Palance said confidently.

Gerry shrugged. "All right, Palance, so you guessed it. I was going to wait until the radiation outside had dropped a couple of more points, then we. . . ."

"You and Kay?"

"Who else?"

Some of the tension was gone from Palance now, as he gestured towards the big gray metal locker. "And the suits are in there?"

Gerry nodded. "You want me to take you along, instead of Kay—is that it?"

"Unless you'd rather I killed you and went alone," Palance said.

"Always provided you know the combination of the lock on the bunker, and where to find the keys to the flyer when you get in there," Gerry said.

Palance showed his teeth briefly. "All right, G.C., so you're still ahead. Why worry? The way I see it, there's no reason why we shouldn't work together. We can be useful to each other. When you get to Dome City you may find things have changed. Certainly if you're planning any kind of takeover, you'll be able to use a man who knows the way you operate—a man you can trust. . . ."

"True." Gerry savoured the grotesque humor in the fact that Palance was capable of making such a speech, while at the same time holding him at the point of a gun. "But what about Mitchell and the others?"

Palance grinned his triumph. "Stop it, G.C., you're breaking my heart." He glanced towards the locker. "Lucky for us both that you like your women tall. That suit should fit me fine. You got the keys?"

"Here you are," Gerry said smoothly. He stood up and reached into his trouser pocket. "Look, if we are going to work together, don't you think it's about time you put that gun down? It makes me nervous."

"You—nervous? That's a laugh," Palance said. "You know something, G.C.? I'd have hated to use it on you. In a kind of a way you remind me of myself." He put the gun on the desk and took the key from Gerry's outstretched hand. "You know, I think we understand each other better because of this. We're both ruthless bastards, but we can work together. When we get to Dome City. . . ." Palance was almost prattling now, as he moved towards the locker, complacent in the knowledge of his victory. He thrust the key into the lock and turned it.

The door was just beginning to swing outwards when Gerry shot him, twice through the back of the neck in rapid succession. The impact of the bullets slammed Palance against the locker, shutting the door. Then his body crumpled slowly to the floor, and the door swung open again.

Inside, the single dark-gray antiradiation suit hung stiffly on its hanger like the flayed skin of some anthropomorphic monster. A helmet with a darkened glass vision plate lay on the floor of the locker, and next to it, a pack containing an air filter mechanism and oxygen supply.

Gerry looked down at the body of Palance. The man would surely have killed him if he had guessed that the locker contained only one antiradiation suit. The other was now part of the charred wreckage in Kay's apartment. Palance, who thought he was so much smarter than the others, hadn't stopped to consider the effect that confinement within an antiradiation suit would have on someone with Kay's asthmatic/claustrophobic symptoms.

She had tried, God how she had tried, in a dozen dry runs, conducted with the two of them alone together in her apartment. And each time Gerry had to remove the helmet for her within less than a minute to reveal her blue-faced, choking for breath, in the throes of yet another attack.

With incredible courage, she had insisted on making at least one attempt each day, arguing that eventually her rebellious mind would be forced by habituation to accept the

11

reality of confinement within the suit. He had been forced to watch her suffer again and again, realizing how hopeless the situation was, deliberately hiding from her his growing conviction that their planned escape together was now impossible, because he knew that if she came to the same conclusion, she would insist that he should go alone. He was determined not to leave her, arguing to himself that within six months or so the radioactivity level outside would have dropped sufficiently to allow them to leave the shelter without antiradiation suits.

Now that Kay was dead he was able to recognize such arguments for the self-delusory rationalizations they really were. Practical indications showed that before the radiation in this immediate area could be expected to die to such a safety level the supplies inside the shelter would have long been exhausted. Elsewhere it might be different, but to travel elsewhere it would have been necessary for Kay to wear an antiradiation suit for some time. If the fire had not happened, they might have been able to survive for fifteen months, even longer—if he had been able to forage successfully outside. But eventually there could have been only one possible end to such a situation. Even so, they would at least have been together, now. . . .

A knock on the door disturbed his thoughts. He closed the locker and turned the key before shouting: "Come in!"

The newcomer was Buzz Mitchell, his eyes red-rimmed and bleary as he gazed from Gerry to the crumpled body of Palance.

"You all right, G.C.?"

Gerry realized that he was still holding Palance's gun. "Sure, I'm fine. Your playmate here started getting big ideas and pulled this thing on me."

Mitchell grunted. "Mean bastard—never did trust him. Always did figure he'd outsmart himself one of these days."

Gerry thrust the gun into his trouser pocket. For once Mitchell's dullness was a positive asset, he seemed to have accepted the situation without question. "Did Inman hear the shots?"

"I don't think so. He took that old bag of his into the generator room a while back."

12

"Good!" Gerry said. "In that case you'd better give me a hand to get this filth into the entrance lock. I can dump him outside when I go foraging."

"Sure, G.C., anything you say," Mitchell said.

The following morning the three of them, Inman, his wife, and Mitchell, stood watching complacently as Gerry, wearing the antiradiation suit, closed the inner door of the lock behind him. He calmed the naggings of conscience by reminding himself that he owed them no debt. They had, after all, a better chance of survival than most people remaining alive at that time.

Outside, although it was still early June, no birds sang in the branches of trees whose leaves were shriveled and brown. Within ten minutes he was aboard the flyer, skimming westward over a lifeless landscape gripped in the unnatural silence of a false, man-made autumn.

CHAPTER TWO

"All right, I've seen enough." Moule turned away from the desolate landscape which was gradually unfolding on the encephalo-screen.

Michael Davidson switched down the sound volume. Tall, with thinning fair hair and long bony features that might have been expressly designed to register anxiety, he faced the squat Control Director, tension jerking at his limbs. "You approve of the program?"

Moule grunted. "I suppose so, but I must say that, as one of the more vociferous members of the antiviolence lobby, you have a remarkable talent for creating gratuitously nasty fantasies."

"I was merely making use of the natural tendencies of Clyne's character," Davidson said, with a carefully calculated touch of indignation.

"I take it that he arrives at Dome City without further major incident?" Moule said calmly. He was an ugly man of indeterminate age, with a round, bald head jammed down between broad shoulders so that no neck was distinguishable. His body gave the impression of having been created under some extraordinary pressure, and this effect was furthered by arms and legs of elephantine solidity. Only in the eyes, which were of an unusually pale amber, was there any tempering of the overall grossness. At times these were gentle, almost feminine, in their sensitivity. "The program will serve its purpose well enough," he said. "But that doesn't mean I'm happy about it. Why, for instance, did you cast Laura Frayne in the role of Clyne's wife?"

"One has to use the more readily available images," Davidson said. "Such methods are common practice."

"Even so, I find something rather disturbing in this case. The burning scene in particular seems to indicate to me that you are developing dangerously obsessional tendencies."

"It was a necessary part of the dramatic framework," protested Davidson. "If a Programmer is to be judged by. . . ."

"All right, Michael. No doubt you are capable of producing valid rationalizations of the entire sequence," Moule said. "But just let me ask you this—how long did you spend on the memory/fantasy of the relationship between Clyne and Kay?"

"As part of the character programming it had to be explored in detail."

"Possibly . . . but I hardly think it was necessary to go quite so deeply into specifically sexual areas of experience," Moule said.

"I disagree. Hypersexuality is part of the syndrome in an aggressive paranoid of Clyne's type. I had to explore the areas in question if I was to understand the subject's dramatic needs."

"A task which you evidently performed with considerable zeal," Moule said. "Well, I suppose there's no harm done, provided that Clyne doesn't come into actual contact with Laura Frayne. If he were to do so it could provide an unnecessarily explosive situation as far as he is concerned, and an embarrassing one for her."

"It could, but such a situation isn't likely to arise, is it?"

14

"Let's hope not," Moule said thoughtfully. "By the way, when is your next Psyche Profile check due?"

"About a month's time," Davidson said. "Why, are you suggesting. . . ?"

"I'm not suggesting anything," Moule replied calmly. "The work of a Programmer is highly demanding, and it carries great responsibility. Such checks are for your own protection."

Davidson watched guardedly as the Control Director moved ponderously across the room towards the couch where the subject lay, the top part of his head hidden by the gleaming silver bowl of the Programming Induction Unit. Clyne's eyes were closed and his face unnaturally pale under the anaesthetic effect of the field which enveloped his brain, but even in this condition there was a look of power about the fleshily handsome face, with its full mouth and jutting, dark-shadowed jaw.

Moule said, "I didn't pick up any reference to the machine pistol in the runthrough."

"I included it as part of the standard equipment of Clyne's flyer, along with two hundred rounds of spare ammunition."

Moule nodded. "Good. Brenner's people are getting pretty low, and Ulanov has been pressing hard recently."

"I would have thought it better to do something through Meyer."

"To damp things down?" Moule turned his amber eyes on the Programmer. "Haven't you seen Meyer's reports? Ask Laura to run one through for you some time. I'm beginning to doubt whether he will even be capable of functioning as an efficient observer much longer, let alone influencing Ulanov on matters of policy. No, Clyne will help even up the balance. He's a classic case—ruthless, aggressive, and smooth enough with it to have managed to stay out of the hands of the department for over thirty-five years."

"From what I've seen of the inside of his mind, he was never *that* smooth," said Davidson. "It's obvious from his record that he's been a sociopath of the most dangerous kind for many years. But a man who makes his first million by the age of twenty-seven doesn't have to worry too much about routine Socio-Psyche checks, does he?"

15

"Go on," Moule said quietly, still looking down at Clyne.

"It seems clear to me that Clyne must have had some considerable pull in certain quarters. His is a familiar situation in cases of this type. The subject goes on getting away with one social crime after another, gradually building up a greater and greater contempt for the Code, until finally he commits some act that just can't be squared. At that point, however costly it may be for them, his powerful friends are forced either to withdraw their protection or reveal their interest. Usually, as a matter of self-preservation, they take the first alternative and the subject goes for Erasure and Reconditioning, or is sent here to us."

"Where he is provided with an environment within which he can work out his sociopathic aggressions," said Moule.

Davidson's bony features betrayed his inner agitation as he said: "And may very well die as a result of the situation you have created within the Controlled Environment."

Moule remained impassive. "Even when that happens —and you must admit that it is a rarity—it can be no worse from the point of view of the subject than the so-called 'little death' of Erasure, which breaks the continuity of individual consciousness just as surely as the real thing."

Davidson could feel the tightening of the muscles in his gut. If only once, just once, he could get through Moule's stolid exterior and elicit an angry response. "All right, so we preserve continuity. But there still isn't any real point, because we never send anybody back."

"You mean we haven't sent anybody back *yet*," corrected Moule. "That is because our function at this stage is a research, rather than a therapeutic one. Every day, through observation of Inside, we are learning more about the sociopathic aspects of personality."

"Possibly, but I don't consider that as sufficient justification for us to go on indefinitely encouraging these wretched people to go on killing and maiming each other, fighting like mad cats confined in a sack.

Moule shook his head with infuriating calm. "My dear Michael, you allow yourself to become too deeply involved emotionally—a fault which shows its results in both your professional and private life. Surely, as a scientist you must

16

appreciate that we have a unique opportunity here, one never before available to any researchers into the nature of the human psyche."

"Either that, or we have the cruelest, most blatant piece of God-playing ever carried out by human beings on members of their own species," Davidson said.

The Director's pale eyes remained gentle. "An interesting point of view," he said, thoughtfully. "You seem to be implying that this whole establishment is being run to satisfy my personal whim; that I'm like some mad Roman emperor, convincing himself of his own deity through the exercise of the power of life and death over thousands of wretched slaves. The truth is rather less dramatic, as you are fully aware. What happens Inside is merely a logical extrapolation on the principles of Existential Analysis laid down by Laing over a century and a half ago, carried out under carefully controlled conditions."

"A technique whose value was not finally acknowledged at that time, or since," Davidson said.

"I happen to believe that it holds a greater hope for the mentally sick members of our race than the quasisurgical process of Reconditioning which treats the human mind as if it were a jigsaw puzzle from which pieces can be removed and replaced at will," Moule said. "That is surely nearer to this God-playing of which you accuse me?" He glanced at the wall-clock. "I must be going. I'll leave you to arrange the transportation details." He moved towards the door.

"Yes, Director," Davidson said, realizing that there was no point in attempting to pursue the argument further. They had once again reached a familiar *impasse*. In principle he could do little other than agree with Moule; it was the man's methods he abhorred. He recognized that there was some truth in the suggestion about his own emotional overinvolvement, it was a tendency he had tried to curb in himself, but sooner or later his overintensity always seemed to trap him into some situation that demonstrated once again his own vulnerability. He saw himself as playing with life like a matador, incapable of withdrawing from the ring when prudence suggested he should do so, because of his commitment—staying on, making progessively more dangerous passes, until finally he was gored yet again. His relationship with Laura Frayne was a typical example of such a situation. Her very indifference was a magnet which made him pursue her all the more, demanding her attention, if only in order that she should flay him with a despising glance.

There was little doubt that Moule's implied analysis of the burning incident in Clyne's programming was close to the truth. His use of a projection of Laura in the role of Kay was a clear attempt to gain some kind of revenge for the humiliation he had suffered at her hands: a dangerously psychotic one, if interpreted literally. His cheeks and mind burned as unwanted memory returned unbidden. It might have been easier if Laura had been a romantic ideal, unattainable—but to have possessed her fully, and *then* be rejected, this was the truly bitter part of the affair, one which he savored again and again like gall, every time he allowed himself to think of her. . . .

With an effort of will, he wrenched his thoughts away from the well-trodden path of self-examination and occupied himself with the remaining tasks concerned with the finalization of Clyne's programming. In this, at least, he was determined to demonstrate his potency in a manner that Laura, Moule, and all the rest of them could not fail to recognize. There was some satisfaction in the knowledge that under his control, Clyne would be a weapon capable of destroying the reality which Moule had created Inside.

The sociopaths with whom the project dealt were highly individual, intelligent people. In one respect, at least, Moule was right. Erasure and Reconditioning was not the answer, entailing as it did the cancelling out of the very factors which made them individuals, and reeducating the resultant *tabula rasa* of mind along approved, innocuous lines—a process that turned them into socially useful, conforming robots, rather than real human beings. Erasure and Reconditioning was the most generally accepted method of treating sociopaths, because it produced the conformity which was regarded logically by those in authority as essential for the smooth functioning of an overcrowded, overorganized society. What those same authorities failed to recognize was that most of the advances which had led to the creation of Earth's present society must have been conceived, in the first place,

18

by just the kind of individual spirits it now worked so hard to extinguish.

The situation had historical parallels. When men were pushing back the frontiers of Earth, opening up new territories against all manner of dangers, the strong individual, quick with his weapons, the killer, was necessary for the survival of the community. But as that society became less primitive, and danger from outside lessened, the same characteristics that had made such men its natural defenders turned them into murderers and criminals; enemies of the community. In fact, it was not the men who had changed, but the nature of the community, which had become static, rather than expanding. In this sense, the entire human race had now become a static community, with 99.9 percent of its members living on an overcrowded Earth, despite the fact that the other planets of the solar system were, theoretically at least, available for colonization. Perhaps the situation might have been different if the planets had proved more naturally hospitable to human life, but even the hostile environments they presented would not have deterred colonization if there had been sufficient pioneering spirit left alive in men.

As it was, the enormous dome which was to have been the home of the first Earth colony on Mars had lain unused for over fifty years, awaiting colonists who never arrived because of a combination of administrative bungling, bad public relations, and apathy. It had remained that way until some seven years previously, when the Socio-Psyche Department had begun looking for a suitable site for the proposed Controlled Environment Project. Spurred on by the fact that it was manifestly impossible to find a habitable, but isolated area of the kind needed on overcrowded Earth, an investigatory party was sent to Mars.

There it was found that the builders of the old colonial dome had done their work better than even they could have realized. Self-repairing, with its own computer-controlled weather system, the forty-square-mile interior of the dome was now a lush subtropical ecological system in which the originally introduced flora and fauna had thrived and multiplied. There on desert Mars, a new Garden of Eden awaited mankind, more than fulfilling the promises which had sought

19

unsuccessfully so many years before to lure colonists away from the familiar security of Earth.

The department proceeded in its usual efficient, self-effacing manner. Within six months another, smaller, dome had been built near to the original, and linked to it by an elaborate communications system. This system made it possible for watchers in the new Control dome to monitor everything that went on in the original dome, which came to be called amongst those concerned in the project simply —Inside. In addition to the monitoring network, Control was connected with Inside by a subway system, so that when physical intervention was necessary within the environment, role-players could be introduced at any one of a dozen different, carefully concealed points.

Even if the subway entrances had not been hidden, it was doubtful if any of the subjects of the Controlled Environment would have attempted to use them.

The programming implanted in their minds before they were introduced to the Inside environment left them with the unbreakable conviction that nothing but radioactive wasteland, in which it would be impossible to survive, lay outside the dome. In this respect the programming of all inhabitants of Inside was identical, but beyond that there was a great deal of variation. Each case had to be handled individually by a Programming specialist using as his basis a detailed study of the mind of the subject. Programming was a delicate process, still more of an art than a science, in that a great deal had to be left to the discretion of the Programmer, and his personal interpretation of the material thus placed at his disposal.

A certain amount of erasure was necessary, removing the immediate memories of the subject relating to the circumstances of his arrest by officers of the Socio-Psyche Department and his subsequent classification as a dangerous sociopath; but compared with the depth of erasure employed in the process of Erasure and Reconditioning this was a minor interference with the structure of mind, analogous to the way in which a dentist drills, but leaves the major part of a tooth and its roots intact as a basis on which to build a new crown. It was then the task of the Programmer to build up a personalized variation on the basic story of atomic disaster, and a corroborating rationalization of the means by which the subject came to find himself Inside—a means which had to be adapted to bring itself into line with both his character and his existing hinterland of memory.

When such links had been forged by an expert Programmer the subject accepted his situation Inside without question, and invariably acted in accordance with the false memories that had been implanted in his mind. In this respect it had been found that the very structure of mind itself was on the side of the Programmers, because like nature, mind abhors a vacuum, and weaves a web of rationalization over the blank spots left by partial erasure, in the same way that a body heals itself by the production of scar tissue. This process reinforced the subjective truth of the new reality that had been introduced into the mind of the subject, and made him even more prepared to accept as part of his own experience the tape created by the Programmer.

A green light on the panel in front of Davidson flickered on, indicating that the replay of the tape was completed. Glancing towards the screen, which was linked with Clyne's visual perception centers, to show his subjective view of the events fed into his mind, Davidson was shocked to see the face of the woman Clyne would now remember as Kay. Tall and slim, with short, artfully tousled honey-blonde hair and a wide mouth that always seemed to be on the edge of a smile. Clear and unmistakable, this was the image that had floated spontaneously to the surface of Clyne's dreaming mind.

With a quick movement, Davidson switched off the screen. But the after-image lingered in his own mind, as he moved to the couch and, with shaking hands, began to remove the silver bowl of the Induction Unit from Clyne's head.

CHAPTER THREE

Laura Frayne paused outside the door of Michael Davidson's apartment. Both experience and intuition told her that she had been a fool to come in response to his vid-call. Over the past couple of months she should have had ample experience to make her wary, and yet again and again, probably because of some hidden guilt feelings about the way she had treated Davidson, she found herself walking with wide-open eyes into situations like this.

Her hands clenched as she realized that what she was really waiting for was a director, to give her a briefing on the scene she was about to play—to suggest what her emotional tone should be, and her opening lines. But there was no director. This was real life, not a Senso-Drama set. There were no cuts, and perhaps most important of all, no retakes. You fluffed a line in this drama and there was no way of altering it. Life was life was life. . . .

And sometimes life was hell. Her work in Control was rewarding in some respects, but there were times when she awoke in the small, dark hours, speculating on the might-have-been continuation of her other career.

Until *Eastern Flame* she had been a little-known young actress, playing supporting roles. At the outset it had seemed that the role of Natasha in Berghoff's latest production was nothing more than a continuation of the gentle upward curve of her professional progress. The role of the girl soldier as originally sketched in the draft script was a minor one which might well end on the cutting-room floor, despite whatever life she was able to inject into it.

Its fate might have been just that, had it not been for a chain of coincidences, the first of which was a case of hate at first sight between Kurt Jagerman and Helen Pomeroy, the two romantic leads. Even before the beginning of rehearsals it was obvious that a love-affair between these two had about as much chance of getting off the ground as a dead ostrich. In the old movie/TV days it might have been possible to get around such a difficulty—in fact, if the old biographical tapes and films were to be believed, such a situation was quite common. But Senso-Drama demanded more, much more than the mere outward simulation of emotion from the lead characters.

Berghoff was planning to issue *Flame* in the usual two versions, one male and one female; the male using the viewpoint and sensory reactions of Jagerman, in his role as Karanin, the Soviet general; the female, that of Helen Pomeroy, as the North American ambassadress, Carmelita O'Rourke. The production was to be a typical Berghoff epic; huge supporting cast and tremendous sets, but with the intimate counterpoint of the passionate love-affair between Karanin and the ambassadress. In this respect there could be no faking, or dubbing—it had to be the real thing, or nothing. In other productions, a certain amount of preconditioning was sometimes fed into the mind of one or both of the viewpoint characters. It was rumored, for instance, that Gaston Morel had to be preconned for his lead role in *Star Wanderer*; but then, considering the theme, and Gaston's legendary heterosexuality, there was a valid reason in that case. But Berghoff refused to use such artificial aids. He demanded complete emotional participation from his actors, insisting that the sensory quality of the recording was impaired by any kind of preconditioning. It was his credo that Senso-Drama should present complete emotional and physical truth, and that this could only be achieved by sincere participation on the part of the viewpoint players.

It was obvious from the first script brainstorming session that Pomeroy and Jagerman were completely antipathetic, and Pomeroy in a TV interview with Bipsy Gordon had aggravated the situation by declaring herself unwilling even to consider the idea of preconditioning. An added discordant factor was Jagerman's failure to conceal his evident attraction towards Laura during the first prerehearsal session.

Laura was aware of her own positive response to Jagerman's interest, but she made every attempt at that stage to hide her feelings. As a small part player, she knew the danger of offending Pomeroy, who was notorious for demanding the head of any person lower in the pecking order who crossed her path. Brainstorming sessions were nominally democratic, with everyone entitled to put forward uninhibited opinions, but Berghoff was, after all, Berghoff. Pomeroy, giving way to an unusually violent fit of bitchiness—even for her—overplayed her hand by demanding story-line changes that were completely in conflict with Berghoff's preconceptions of his epic. The resultant collision

23

culminated in the sweeping walkout of Helen Pomeroy, as she delivered a curtain line that made even the hardened script editors blush.

The rest, in the annals of Senso-Drama, was history. Nobody who walked out on Berghoff was ever given the opportunity of walking in again. Pomeroy was out for good. But as a result Berghoff was faced with the problem of expensive studio space booked for three months ahead, with two hundred actors and four times that number of technicians under contract. This being so, it was not surprising that he clutched eagerly at a suggestion proposed by Kurt Jagerman.

Jagerman's idea was that the story-line should be changed and Laura's part of Natasha built up into that of the female romantic lead, with the role of the North American ambassador filled by a male character actor. The production went ahead on these lines, and the final result, after five months of shooting and nearly four of editing was acknowledged as Berghoff's masterpiece, the peak of his career, compared by one historically-minded critic with Griffith's *Birth of a Nation*. The love scenes between Laura and Jagerman were hailed as a new high in emotional and sensory experience, and Laura suddenly found herself acclaimed as the leading female Senso-Drama star of her era. In that respect, her rise to stardom was a cliché, the success dream of every young actress. Afterwards she was to tell herself that such a swiftly inflated bubble had to burst eventually, but at the time it seemed to be an experience which must change the course of her entire life.

This was true, but not quite in the way she had anticipated. The trouble really began quite soon after the rating figures began to come in. These clearly indicated that the Natasha version of *Flame* was outselling the Karanin version by over three-to-one, even among male Senso-Drama buffs, an almost unheard-of phenomenon. Vanity is the actor's besetting sin, and Kurt Jagerman had his full share, so it was not really surprising that he began to resent the sudden ascendancy over himself of this unknown girl whom he had helped to raise from bit-player to stardom—albeit mainly for reasons of his own lust.

The relationship between them went sour with incredible

swiftness. Jagerman walked out on her after a scene which practically wrecked the luxury penthouse they had been sharing, leaving Laura a shivering, near-catatonic wreck. Her maid discovered her in this condition some hours later, and had the presence of mind to call Berghoff, who made immediate arrangements for her to be rushed to Vanbrugh Lawn, the continent's most exclusive private Psyche clinic. There she was given the best treatment money could buy. Theoretically, when she was discharged three months later she should, after a reasonable period of convalescence, have been able to plunge back into the career which Berghoff had already mapped out for her—commencing with a sequel to *Flame*, and after that a new historical epic loosely based on Shakespeare's *Antony and Cleopatra*. But in fact, despite the reassurances of her Psyche specialists, she found herself terrified by the prospect to such an extent that she was physically incapable of setting foot inside a Senso-Drama studio.

This terror was so deep-rooted that it was finally acknowledged that other than treatment by complete Erasure and Reconditioning her case was a hopeless one. And such treatment was out of the question, because it would have meant her reemergence as a completely different personality from the one which had made her such a success as a Senso-Drama star.

Faced by this situation she reacted with characteristic courage, making a decision which preserved the integrity of her personality, and at the same time gave her life a renewed sense of purpose. Abandoning all thought of continuing her career as an actress, she enrolled for a course of training at the Socio/Psyche Institute, from which she emerged after four years as a fully-qualified Psycho-drama specialist. Soon afterwards, she applied for a vacancy on the staff of the Mars Controlled Environment Project. Since that time she had worked in the department which dealt with the training and control of personnel who were sent Inside as Role-Players. Her previous experience in Senso-Drama, plus her dedication, had made her such a success in this work that for the past year she had been head of the department.

However, despite the new awareness of the workings of

personality which her Socio/Psyche training had given her, she was still to some degree emotionally accident-prone in her relationships with the male sex. Undoubtedly the traumatic scars of the Jagerman episode still existed deep down in her psyche, but she suspected that the real source of the trouble lay even deeper, a compulsion that made it impossible for her to form a steady, lasting relationship with any man. This being the case, there had been several affairs during her time on Mars, each of which had broken up after a time without too much soul-searching—until she had become involved with Michael Davidson. . . .

It was not until too late that she realized Michael was incapable of accepting such a breakup. Instead of taking her decision that their relationship should come to an end in a rational, civilized manner, he had reacted by creating a violently emotional scene, accusing her of deliberate cruelty in rejecting his love.

Love . . . It now became apparent that their concepts of the emotion differed radically. Rightly or wrongly, she had come to look upon love as the sharing of physical pleasure accompanied by a certain mutual affection. This seemed to her a rational definition of a relationship which could not, because of the limiting factors in her own nature, be a permanent one. For Michael Davidson, on the other hand, she found that the word meant something completely different. Love to him was a weapon, a means of possessing another person, of imprisoning them within walls of emotion.

Each time he had managed to get her on her own during the last couple of months he had reproached her, begged her, threatened her, according to his mood; and each time she had concluded the encounter by reiterating her decision that the relationship was at an end. She pitied him, but the very fact of that pity made the possibility of continuing any physical relationship repulsive to her. Damn it! you couldn't go on forever sleeping with a man because you felt sorry for him . . . And what kind of a man was it that would be prepared to accept such a situation, anyway?

When he had called her half an hour before and asked her to come to his apartment, her first reaction had been to give him a flat refusal and break the connection. But there had been something about his expression, about the way he had said: "Come, Laura, I need your help. I can't explain on the vid." It was an appeal, but in a different mode from his usual pleading.

She pressed the door button, telling herself that she would leave immediately at the first sign of emotional blackmail.

"Laura—it was good of you to come so quickly," he said, smiling as she entered. "Do sit down. What can I get you —the usual?"

She watched him cautiously as she lowered herself into one of the room's two rust-colored chairs. As he walked across to the wall dispenser the change that had been evident in his manner on the vid-screen was more noticeably apparent. There was a new firmness in his voice, and a decisiveness about every movement.

He handed her one of the frosted, ice-clinking glasses, then sat down opposite her. "You're wondering why I asked you to come?"

She nodded, still marvelling at the disappearance of the old querulousness, the new air of control.

"I've put the first stage of the plan into operation," he said quietly. "A man named Clyne. Pelissier's men will be taking him into the Northern sector now."

"The plan—but I thought. . . ." She stared at him in shock.

"You thought that it was just so much talk?"

"Well, no, but. . . ."

"Now why not admit it? You never really believed that I would have the guts to take the plunge, did you? You thought I was just a paper revolutionary like the rest of them."

There was no point in denying what he said. The group who disagreed with Moule's manner of running the Inside environment had tried many times to make their point of view heard at Socio/Psyche Department headquarters on Earth, but such appeals had proved useless. As far as the department was concerned, Moule was director of the Mars Controlled Environment Project, and as such his authority was not to be questioned. Faced with this blank wall of official obstinacy, the group had been forced to recognize that if any change was

27

to be made in the running of Inside it would have to be brought about by their own actions. One possibility was that they should depose Moule and take over the conduct of the project themselves, but this had considerable potential disadvantages. Technically it would constitute an act of mutiny which would assuredly bring about the physical intervention of Earth government forces. Even though they might finally be able to justify the rectitude of their motives and action, there was sure to be a long legal wrangle, during which time nothing would be done to change the situation Inside.

Agreed upon the disadvantages of such a course, they had finally accepted a suggestion from Davidson that, rather than tackle the problem through Moule, they should bring about the desired changes in the dramatic pattern of events Inside by introducing two individuals into the environment whose programming had been especially modified. These subjects, one introduced into the Northern Sector and the other into the Southern would have to be possessed of highly dominant personalities, natural leaders, each of whom was capable of forcing his will on one of the two groups that constituted the population of Inside, and yet at the same time could be controlled when necessary. Some of the group had expressed doubts about the possible difficulties of maintaining control over two such personalities, but finally, after much argument, Davidson's repeated assurances that these problems could be overcome by careful Programming won the day, and in the absence of any feasible alternative, the plan was accepted.

Accepted in principle, that was. Laura found herself wondering just what the reaction of the less enthusiastic members of the group would be when they heard that Davidson had already placed the first phase of the plan in motion.

"Have you spoken to any of the others about this yet?" she asked.

Davidson shook his head. "No—I wanted to talk with you first, because the major manipulations involved will necessarily depend on the two of us. I have programmed Clyne and I should be able to control him, but the cooperation of the Role-Players, Torrance in particular, will be essential."

"But Torrance knows nothing of the plan," Laura objected. "If he did. . . ."

"He would probably go straight to Moule and expose us? Yes, I've already considered that. But bear in mind that the introduction of Clyne into the environment is only the first step. There remains a great deal to be done before he is in a position to produce the required effect in the Northern Sector, and before that happens we must also introduce his opposite number in the Southern Sector and establish him. Initially we shall have to work through Torrance, making sure that he provides Clyne with the necessary introductions and gives him a working knowledge of the new social situation."

"And all this is to be done without producing any hint of suspicion in the mind of Torrance?" Laura said doubtfully. "Torrance is no fool. If this Clyne is as strong a personality as you suggest, I hardly think that Torrance will fail to recognize him as a potential menace to the status quo."

"Then you, as his section head, will have to suggest to him that Moule is fully aware of the possibilities inherent in the introduction of Clyne."

"And if he still questions the situation?"

"Whilst he is Inside, Torrance can only communicate with Moule through the reports he makes to you," Davidson pointed out.

"Falsification of reports, erasures and editings, will only be possible for so long," Laura said

"I appreciate that, but then such measures may only be necessary for a short time. Once the situation Inside is changed there will be nothing Moule can do about it, short of reprogramming each individual within the environment —and without our cooperation that would be quite impossible."

"It seems reasonable. . . ."

"Of course it's reasonable," Davidson said sharply. "We are all agreed that some change must be made, and this is the way it will be done, provided you and I play our parts correctly." He glanced at the wall-clock. "The others will be arriving in half an hour. Some of them are sure to dither and make excuses, but if you back me they'll have to cooperate. What do you say?''

"I'd like more time to think about it. . . .''

"Think! What's to think about? The plan has been discussed and agreed, and now I've put it into action.''

Laura looked into his lean, intense features. The plan *had* been discussed and agreed—in principle—but she had a strong suspicion that the agreement had been reached as a substitute, rather than as a plan, for action; that having made at least some decision, the majority of the group were now quite content to leave the matter there. She found herself wondering just what the reaction of the others would be when they found their complacency shattered by Davidson's presentation of a *fait accompli*.

"All right, Michael—I'll support you,'' she said quietly.

CHAPTER FOUR

The room was about eight meters square. The door through which he had entered was now closed, and another lay open ahead of him. Gerry Clyne shrugged off a brief spell of dizziness and concentrated on listening to the voice that issued from a loudspeaker placed high on the pale gray wall to his right.

"You will remove outer clothing, underwear, and shoes, and place them in the Clothing Hatch. Items other than clothing should be placed in the hatch marked EFFECTS. These will be processed and returned to you after you have passed through the final stage of decontamination. If these instructions are not clear to you please refer to the wall chart on the left of the Clothing Hatch. This explains decontamination procedure in detail. You will not—I repeat *not*, be allowed to proceed through decontamination unless you comply with these instructions.''

He guessed that there would be no point in questioning the orders. The decontamination unit was completely automated, the voice a prerecorded tape set in motion by his entry. He laid the machine pistol and ammunition pack on the floor and began to strip. The interior of the antiradiation suit was becoming more like a sauna bath every minute, and it was a relief to feel the atmosphere of the room pleasantly cool against his naked body. The plastic-surfaced floor was comfortably yielding to his bare feet. The planners, it seemed, had thought of everything.

There was very little in the pockets of his clothing; a wallet containing identification and some money—quite useless now, of course, belonging to that no longer existent premissile war world—a wrist watch, a half-empty packet of cigarettes and a butane lighter. Carrying these items, he moved to the Effects hatch.

Pulling the handle downwards revealed an inner compartment about a meter square, apparently constructed on the commonly used bank Night Safe pattern. He placed the wallet and other things inside, and released his grip on the handle, allowing the counter-balanced shutter to move upwards again, hiding the contents from view.

Bundling clothing and boots together, he thrust them into the other hatch. Then he bent down and picked up the machine pistol, looping the strap of the ammunition pack over his naked shoulder. He headed for the open doorway.

He was about half a meter away when a klaxon began its raucous outcry and the door slid across swiftly, slamming shut with positive force.

The klaxon ceased, and the loudspeaker began to repeat its previous message.

"You will remove all outer clothing, underwear, and. . . ."

The message was clear. It had been in the first instance, but his own stubbornness and the hope of discovering some loophole had prompted him to avoid carrying out its orders to the letter.

". . . allowed to proceed through decontamination unless you comply with these instructions." The emotionless voice ceased.

He hesitated, feeling the comforting bulk of the gun in his right hand. The voice had promised that all effects would be returned after processing, but could he rely on that promise?

31

It was possible that the foresighted planners had decided in their wisdom that all weapons should be confiscated. There was no possibility of advance as long as he retained the weapon, but there was no going back now, either, nothing to go back to, especially without his clothing. . . .

He walked back to the Effects hatch and reopened it. The wallet and other things were gone. He lifted the ammunition pack from his shoulder and placed it inside, allowing the hatch to close again.

He looked back at the door. It was still shut. A rage of frustration growing in him, he glared up at the loudspeaker, his hands automatically raising the machine pistol, then lowering it again as the rational part of his brain reminded him that it was stupid to lose one's temper with unthinking gadgetry. Lowering the weapon, he reopened the hatch. The ammunition pack was gone.

Consoling himself with the thought that a similar defeat must have been suffered by every human being who had attempted to pass this way with a weapon, he put the gun in the hatch and released the handle. In any case, even with nothing to defend himself other than his powerful body and his intelligence, he fancied that he was still not exactly helpless.

This time there was no klaxon. The door slid open and he walked through into a second chamber where he found himself facing a row of four open cubicles that looked like shower stalls.

There was a loudspeaker on the wall in this room as well. It said: "When the red light comes on, you will step into the cubicle thus indicated and remain there, standing in an upright position, until you receive further instructions."

The light over the second cubicle from the right flickered on. He stepped inside, and immediately became aware of a low-pitched, electronic hum. Cold sweat trickled from his armpits down his bare ribs. There was probably no reason for alarm, but without clothes and weapons he felt somehow doubly naked and vulnerable.

"Instruments built into the walls of the cubicle are now measuring the radioactivity which has been absorbed by your body," said the taped voice. "When this task has been

32

completed, you will be put through a program of cleansing and treatment appropriate to the amount of radiation measured. You are reminded that all measures are taken in your own interest, and that complete cooperation in all phases of this program is essential. Radiation is an invisible killer which can. . . .''

The admonitions of the disembodied voice were unnecessary in the case of Gerry Clyne. He had made his choice. Even though the process seemed at times to be tediously prolonged, he submitted himself meekly to all the cleansings, probings, and testings visited on him by the automated decontamination unit, until finally he arrived at a square, gray room similar to the first, even down to the detail of the two hatches.

By this time he was so used to obeying the orders of the voice that he was able to resist his natural impulse to dive first for the Effects Hatch. Instead, as instructed, he opened up the Clothing Hatch. It contained clean underwear, gray shirt and trousers, and a pair of light, moccasin-type shoes. These were not the clothes he had deposited earlier, but they were surgically clean and his correct size, so he put them on. He would have no need of antiradiation clothing within the dome, neither would he need heavier protection than this in an environment where the temperature was automatically regulated at around twenty-one degrees centigrade.

Dressed, he opened the Effects Hatch. It contained only his wallet, watch, cigarettes, and lighter. So the voice had tricked him after all . . . But it was too late to do anything about it now. He slipped the watch onto his wrist—noting that over two hours had passed—and put the other articles into his pockets.

He was about to turn away and head for the still-closed door which was marked WAY OUT, when an impulse stopped him. He reopened the Effects Hatch.

It contained the ammunition pack, with its precious two hundred rounds . . . Precious? Not without the gun itself. He dragged the pack out and dropped it to the floor—then waited impatiently as the hatch door swung ponderously shut. He pulled it open again, and found the machine pistol inside. It seemed that the processing unit connected with the lockers treated each batch deposited separately and delivered them in the same way. There was, after all, no trickery. The taped voice meant exactly what it had said.

". . . processing is now completed, and you may leave by the main exit. You are . . ."

The voice was no longer important. The ammunition pack slung over his left shoulder, gun grasped firmly in his right hand, he strode for the door, which slid open soundlessly.

Outside the doorway the contrast with the drab, uniform gray of the decontamination unit was startling. He found himself standing on a concrete walkway about three meters wide and flanked on either side by subtropical vegetation, the deep green of which was splashed at random with the glowing colors of flowering plants whose names were not familiar to him. In contrast with the sterile atmosphere of the decontamination unit the air was humid and warm and laden with strangely exotic smells.

About fifty meters ahead the walkway curved to the left, disappearing between the palms and bushes. He was about to walk in that direction when he felt a pressure in the small of his back.

"Drop the gun, friend," said a gravelly voice behind him.

His body rigid, still holding onto the gun, Gerry said: "And if I don't?"

"That's up to you, friend," the voice said with a harsh cheerfulness. "I shall just have to kill you, is all."

Gerry cursed the carelessness that had led him to step straight out of the known environment of the decontamination unit into this unknown without taking any precautions. But there had been no reason to anticipate any danger. If this was an ambush, he found himself wondering as to its purpose. In the kind of shelter he had left to come here, it made sense to keep people out, because the shelter could only house and feed a certain number of people for a definite, limited period. Dome City, on the other hand, had ample supplies, and was further capable of producing . . .

"You hear me?" The rasping query was accented by an increased pressure of the gun muzzle against Gerry's backbone.

"All right, have it your way," he said. Bending forward and down, he placed the gun on the concrete in front of him.

"Fine . . . that's fine, friend," said the other. "Now, take four paces forward, and turn around, nice and slow and easy."

Gerry moved with measured care, and turned. His captor was a big man with short-cropped, copper-red hair and a round face that gave an impression of amiable idiocy until one noticed the greenish-blue, alert eyes. The gray shirt he was wearing was obviously a couple of sizes too small for him, the buttons down its front strained against the pressure of his barrel chest. His gun was an old army pattern 303 rifle, and it was pointed steadily at Gerry's navel.

"Would you mind telling me what this is all about?" asked Gerry.

"For now, I'm asking the questions," said the big man. "Where are you from?"

Gerry told him.

The man seemed unimpressed. "Prove it," he said.

"Look, what the hell difference does it make where I come from?" Gerry said, with growing impatience. "You know what it's like out there. Why would I lie, anyway?"

The big man said a few words in a language that was completely incomprehensible to Gerry.

"For Pete's sake!" Gerry said. "What is this—some kind of gag?"

"No gag, friend," said the redhead. "You answered that last sentence, and maybe I'd have blown your head off anyway. But you didn't, so either you're smart, or you just don't talk Russian."

"Russian—why the hell should I?" demanded Gerry.

"You don't know the answer to that one, then could be you are all right. Anyway, that's not for me to say. My job is to take you in, so the colonel can question you."

"The colonel?"

"Sure, Colonel Brenner."

The name was not familiar to Gerry, but then there was no real reason why it should be. "This Brenner—he's in charge here?"

"You got the picture, friend. And if you want to stay healthy, you better give him the right answers." The big man's eyes flickered down towards the gun which lay on the concrete between them. "Turn around, and don't move."

Gerry shrugged. "If it makes you happy." He turned slowly, the muscles of his powerful body tensing. He knew that he would be risking his life in what he was about to attempt, but he had no intention of submitting meekly to captivity. He stood, listening intently, waiting for the change in the sound of the big man's breathing as he bent to pick up the weapon.

It came at last, an almost imperceptible grunt, but still he forced himself to wait, counting . . . one . . . two . . . *Now*!

He swung round, right leg flinging outwards as he did so. He had a brief vision of the redhead, crouched froglike, then his right foot connected with vicious force to the side of his captor's head. The man sprawled sideways under the impact of the blow, the rifle clattering from his grip onto the concrete.

Before the other had time to recover, Gerry was in possession of the machine pistol, holding it trained steadily. "All right, on your feet," he ordered.

The big man obeyed, one hand rubbing at his bruised temple. "Fast, very fast," he rasped, "but you're going to get yourself killed that way one of these days, friend."

"You may be right," Gerry said. "But first I intend to get some answers. Now—what's this Russian business?"

"You really don't know?"

"Would I be asking, if I did? All I've seen in the last twenty-eight days is the inside of a shelter and a couple of hundred miles of radiation-seared landscape."

"They came in through the south entrance, the same day the missile war started."

"*They*?"

"A commando force of maybe fifty," said the big man. "The colonel figures their high command must have had an idea that Dome City was some kind of combat control center. Seems those tri-di projectors didn't have them fooled after all. They knew something important was going on here, and they were determined to find out what."

"I find it difficult to believe that they would actually send a raiding force this deep into our territory," Gerry said.

The big man grinned. "You just got to be kidding, friend. Sure, nobody knows yet whose finger pressed the first button, but when things really started happening, what more natural than that they should send in a force to check on Dome City? Fifty million of our people and maybe double that number of theirs killed in the first day—you think they'd bother too much about what happened to a few commandos, especially if they hoped they might be striking directly at an important control center?"

"And that force is still in the dome?"

"The major part of it. We've managed to hold them off for the past six months, but they're still around."

Six months . . . Gerry let the temporal inaccuracy pass for the time being. For the moment he was more concerned with the remarkable irony of the situation. Dome City had been designed as a sanctuary within which a number of people might be able to survive just such an atomic disaster as that which had taken place, to allow them to survive and rebuild some kind of peaceful existence. Instead, it seemed that the sanctuary itself had now become a battleground, within which the ultimate war, which had burned itself out in the almost total destruction of the world outside, could be continued on a smaller, more personal scale.

"This Colonel Brenner has been organizing the resistance to them?" he asked.

"You guessed it, friend."

"And your job at the moment is to grab anybody who comes through the decontamination unit, just in case the commies have hit on the idea of infiltrating your territory that way?"

The big man nodded. "You've got to admit it would be a possibility, if they could get hold of enough antiradiation suits."

"Then if they haven't tried it after—six months, did you say?—it means they haven't got any such supply of suits. Don't you think you're wasting your time here—what's your name?"

"Annersley—Bub Annersley," grated the redhead. His

alert, greenish-blue eyes regarded Gerry. "You could be right. Maybe you should talk to Brenner."

"I intend to," said Gerry. "I'm Gerry Clyne, by the way." He pointed downwards. "Pick up your rifle and let's go, Bub."

Annersley's mouth dropped open slightly. "You mean that?"

"Of course. We may meet somebody on the way, and I wouldn't like them to get the idea that there was anything wrong."

Annersley shook his head, a grin on his round, bumpkin face. "I don't know just what you are, Clyne, but I'll say this for you—you got nerve."

"Thanks for the compliment," Gerry said. "Now, let's get moving, shall we?"

CHAPTER FIVE

They remained silent for some moments after Davidson had finished speaking, their faces showing a variety of expressions ranging from shock to outright anger. The irony of the situation was not lost on him. In the past he had often had the impression that this oddly assorted group of revolutionaries would have preferred to go on talking indefinitely rather than actually doing something, and now, faced by the unexpected news that he had set the plan in motion, they had nothing to say.

Boehm, the head of Medical Section, was first to recover, tapirlike nose twitching as he said: "But surely there should have been some consultation before . . . "

"Consultation about *what*?" Davidson cut in sharply, determined to maintain his dominant role. "We agreed that this was the way it would have to be done—that when a suitable subject arrived, the plan would be put into operation. Clyne is a suitable subject."

"In *your* opinion," said Agostino. "According to the

reports I've seen, he's a dangerously aggressive personality with pronounced paranoid tendencies." Short, and inclined to overweight, despite a constant daily dosage of lypolitic drugs, Mario Agostino was in charge of the Psyche Department.

"I've read the reports," Davidson said. "Surely it's obvious that we need someone with just those tendencies?"

"But will you be able to control him?" persisted Agostino. "It seems to me quite probable that the kind of programming you describe may well have the effect of aggravating the paranoid aspect of his personality."

Davidson had little time for the Italian, whom he regarded as soft-bellied and self-indulgent. "Naturally—do you usually blunt your knife before cutting into a steak, or do you sharpen it?"

"Your analogy is faulty," Agostino said. His deep brown eyes appealed to the others. "You must understand that we are not dealing here with a puppet, but with a complex, unpredictable personality. . . ."

"Which can be destroyed, or removed as we see fit, at any stage of the game," cut in Davidson.

"In other words, you consider Clyne as expendable?" Agostino said.

Pelissier, a man with the silvery hair and coconut-ice pink complexion of some archetypal elder statesman, stirred uneasily in his chair. "But surely that's precisely the kind of action we are opposed to in Moule's policy? The destruction of this man Clyne would be a negation of our basic principles."

These damned theoretical revolutionaries, with their precious scruples . . . Davidson kept his anger in check with difficulty. "The situation will not arise. When the time comes for Clyne to be activated, he will play the role I have mapped out for him under my personal supervision."

"You're going Inside?" Agostino said.

"Naturally," Davidson said. "I am the only person capable of keying in his blocked memory patterns. But that will not be for some time yet, until his opposite number has been programmed and established in the Southern Sector. For the present Clyne will be fully occupied with the task of taking over leadership of the Northern community from Brenner. Laura is arranging for Torrance to help him in this.''

"And Moule—what will he be doing whilst this is happening?" asked Boehm.

"He has allowed Brenner to remain in control of the Northern Sector because the man's lack of positive aggression has served to prolong the conflict between north and south, but there will be no reason for him to suppose that the new developments are anything other than accidental. He will be content to observe, without interfering.''

"It seems to me that if Clyne is as aggressive as you say, then surely he will recognize the basic absurdity of a situation where a mere handful of invaders are terrorising and pinning down a body of people who outnumber them by a factor of almost ten-to-one,'' said Boehm. "Once he is in command, he is certain to reorganize the northern forces and attack. Then, instead of the present sporadic campaign, with minimal losses on both sides, we shall have a bloody massacre on our hands, and my section just isn't equipped to handle casualties of that order.''

"There will be no massacre,'' Davidson said. "Before that point is reached, I shall have reactivated Clyne's memory chain. When he becomes aware of the true reality of the situation the conflict Inside will cease altogether.''

"Provided that in the meantime you have been able to introduce this other subject into the Southern Sector, and that he has been able to take over from Ulanov—who, I would remind you, is a very different proposition from Brenner,'' said Agostino.

"You're forgetting that Meyer, Ulanov's second-in-command, is one of our Role-Players,'' Davidson said. "With Laura's help, there is no reason to suppose that the takeover of the Southern Sector should prove any more difficult than that of the north.

Laura frowned. "I don't think we ought to rely too much on Meyer. I'm beginning to think that it may have been a mistake to put him in such a role in the first instance—the combined effect on him of Ulanov's personality and the violence of the environment. . . .''

"Then you will have to recommend his replacement," Agostino said. "We must have someone in a position of influence within the Southern Sector when the second subject is introduced."

Laura said: "At the moment all I have to go on is a feeling about Meyer—there's been no positive sign of a breakup. If I were to put such a recommendation to Moule on the basis of what little evidence I can produce so far, he might start asking questions."

Davidson felt the flush of color rise to his cheeks, as he realized that just when he needed her positive support to overcome the doubting criticism of Agostino, Laura was adopting an attitude of negative uncertainty. "There will be plenty of time to think about that later," he said. "It may be a matter of months before a suitable subject arrives. At least for the moment, we have to concentrate our attention on Clyne."

"How long do you anticipate it will be before Clyne is able to take over?" asked Boehm.

"That must depend to some extent on the amount of help Torrance gives him."

"But surely you will have to be more precise than that?" Boehm said, his dark, long-nosed face clouded with worry.

"If there's too much of a time lag between Clyne's takeover of leadership in the Northern Sector and that of his opposite number in the south, then the only possible result can be a disastrous escalation of the conflict Inside, a situation which—I repeat—might well produce more casualties than my department is capable of processing. Under such circumstances the irretrievable loss of human lives could be considerable."

"If there's any sign of such a situation arising, then we shall have to intervene," Davidson said.

"Precisely," Agostino said, leaning forward in his chair. "And how could we possibly do *that* without arousing Moule's suspicions?"

"No—I think you're wrong there," Laura said. "Provided he accepts Clyne's rise to power as a natural progression of events, there seems no reason to suppose that he would see anything unusual in the necessity of intervention in order to prevent the kind of massacre you suggest. In any case, at this stage such arguments are merely hypothetical. Michael has taken the first step in a plan which, I would remind you, was agreed in principle by all of us here. Under the circumstances I think the least we can do is to support him in every possible way, instead of deliberately anticipating obstacles to the success of that plan."

"I agree with Laura," said Hofer, the head of Electronics Section. A square-faced man in his early thirties with a dark crew-cut, he had sat silent throughout the discussion, but now he rose to his feet and moved over to Davidson's side, turning to face the rest of the meeting. "This job isn't going to be easy, but we all knew that from the beginning, so why start bitching about possible failure now? Michael took one hell of a risk in modifying Clyne's programming. If Moule had the slightest suspicion what had happened, he could have washed Michael out of the Project on the spot and slammed him into custody on the kind of charges that could only result in compulsory Erasure and Reconditioning. The way I see it, Mike has put his money where his mouth is, and it's up to the rest of us to do the same."

Pelissier's silvery head nodded. "You're right, of course, Hofer. There can be no question of our not supporting Davidson's move. My only misgiving lies in the possibility that we may find ourselves forced into using the very methods we set out in the first place to change."

"The time for arguing about ends and means is gone," Laura said, intensely. "Surely you must see that?"

There was a touch of sadness in Pelissier's smile as he looked at her. "Oh for the ruthless idealism of youth . . . Forgive me, my dear. I shall do my best to measure up to your standards."

Conscious that his victory had been won for him by the intervention of Hofer and Laura, Davidson faced the sole remaining dissenter. "Well, Agostino, are you going to be the Judas?"

The fat man rose to his feet with dignity. "I shall support the plan as agreed," he said quietly.

The meeting ended shortly afterwards, and it was only later, alone in his apartment, that Davidson found himself wondering how he could have been so inept as to allow his sense of temporary triumph to lead him into using such a metaphor to the man who was probably the only practicing Christian in the group.

CHAPTER SIX

Gerry Clyne and Annersley paused at the corner of the square. Brenner's headquarters was long, low, and single-storied, with a row of notice boards on either side of a main entrance which was guarded by a uniformed man with a submachine gun. Like the rest of the buildings in this area, which had originally been intended to serve as a temporary work camp during the construction of the city proper, the headquarters was made of light prefabricated sections. Obviously too flimsy to have endured a single storm outside, the entire township was as insubstantial as a house of cards, but quite adequate for the sheltered environment within the dome.

At this moment the guard was looking in the other direction, but Gerry recognized by the alertness of his stance that the man was a seasoned combat veteran. He came to a snap decision.

"All right, Bub. This is where you get to play the hero," he said, turning towards Annersley and handing over the machine pistol.

The big redhead took the weapon automatically, but his mouth gaped. "I don't get it. . . ."

"You don't?" Gerry said. "Look, I'll be safer with you bringing me in that way than I would be walking across the square towards that joker, a total stranger carrying a weapon. I'm not exactly crazy about the idea of getting myself shot."

Annersley shrugged his meaty shoulders. "Makes sense, I got to admit. But how do you know I won't shoot you?"

Gerry grinned. "On the basis of our long acquaintance,

that's a chance I'm willing to take. Let's go, shall we?'' He began to walk forward across the square.

His intuition about the guard proved correct. When they were still over twenty yards away the man turned, raising the submachine gun. ''Who've you got there, Annersley?'' he demanded.

''Outsider—just came in through Decontamination,'' said Annersley.

The man's hard, alert eyes scrutinized Gerry. ''Hold him there while I have a word with the colonel.'' He disappeared inside the building.

''You're a cool bastard,'' Annersley said, with a touch of admiration.

''I used to play a lot of poker,'' Gerry said.

A moment later the guard was back. ''The colonel will see you now.''

Brenner was a slightly built man with sandy, gray-flecked hair and a young/old face dominated by a grotesquely huge and bristling moustache several shades darker.

''Take the gun and ammunition to the weapon store and report back here,'' he said to Annersley.

As his escort left, Gerry Clyne stood easily in front of the light oak desk summing up his first impressions of the man who was apparently in command of the northern sector of the dome. It seemed to him that, like the badges on the neatly pressed uniform shirt, the grotesque moustache was meant to be some kind of symbol of authority. He himself despised the use of such props.

Brenner had a ballpoint in his right hand. ''Name?'' he asked, fish-pale eyes sliding away from Gerry's steady regard.

''Clyne—Gerald Clyne.''

''Where are you from, Clyne?'' Attempting to simulate an abrupt bark of command, the voice ended up somewhere between a querulous yelp and a whine. Gerry knew the signs of insecurity—he had seen them too many times before in small men attempting to hold down jobs that were too big for them. Such men were vulnerable. He gave the requested information briefly.

The ballpoint moved on the pad of paper in front of

44

Brenner. "And how did you get here?" he asked, at length.

"By private flyer. I had one waiting not far from the shelter in case of emergency."

"In fact you planned such an escape in advance?"

"It seemed the sensible thing to do."

Brenner's pale eyes sharpened. "Provided you could be sure that there was somewhere to escape to."

"You're wondering how I knew about the dome?"

"Am I?"

"One of my firms helped in the building—Monarch Engineering," Gerry said. "Ableson, the site manager, should still be here. He'll identify me."

"Perhaps he might have."

"You mean he's gone?"

"You could say that."

Gerry deliberately curbed his growing impatience at what seemed to be turning into some kind of guessing game. "I merely thought it might help if I mentioned someone who could establish my identity."

"Describe this Ableson to me."

Gerry frowned. "He's a big fellow, about six feet three and broad with it. Dark-haired, but losing it fast, and he has a nose that was broken one time and ended up a bit off-center. Used to do quite a bit of amateur boxing when he was younger, and still fancies himself as something of a roughhouse merchant when the occasion arises."

Brenner nodded. "All right, I'm prepared to believe that you knew Ableson."

"*Knew*?"

"He's dead," said Brenner. "It happened six months ago, about a week after the big blowup."

"How?"

"Your friend Ableson was a very stubborn man," Brenner said. "I tried to convince him that there was no point in trying to go on with the building program, that in any case, when his existing supplies ran out, there wouldn't be any more from outside—but he wouldn't listen to reason. He and ten of his men were killed before one of my patrols were able to fight the enemy off."

"I see," Gerry said. "Rough on Ableson."

"Even rougher on the men who were killed because of his stupidity," Brenner said sharply. "He had been warned of the possibility of attack. The responsibility was his."

"And this happened six months ago, you say?"

"Yes—why do you ask?"

"It's just that I was under the impression that it was only just over one month since the missile war," Gerry said, frowning. "I can't see how I could have lost track of time to that extent in the shelter."

"Apparent subjective time differences are quite common in late arrivals from outside," Brenner said. "Torrance, our medic, will give you all the fancy explanations you need; but the main point is that no human being can come through the destruction of an entire civilization without suffering some lasting traumatic effect."

Gerry found the explanation vaguely unsatisfactory, but there was obviously no point in pursuing the subject further with Brenner. In any case, there were matters of more immediate concern to be discussed. "My gun and ammunition—when do I get them back?" he asked.

"That depends on your allocation," Brenner said. "As a civilian, working in food production or maintenance, you would be under the jurisdiction of the Civil Committee, and hardly in need of such a weapon. If, on the other hand, you are allocated to the military branch, and you are assigned to combat duty, then you will be issued with the appropriate armament from the weapon store."

"By the military branch, you mean that I shall be under your command, is that right?" Gerry said.

Brenner nodded. "I can't promise you an easy time. We are faced by a ruthless, highly trained enemy, against whom we must constantly be on our guard. But I have a feeling that a man of your temperament would prefer to do something more active with his life than hoe cabbages."

"I have an option, then?"

"After leaving here you will be interviewed by the Civil Committee. You are allowed to express a preference for which type of service you are prepared to give to the community, and this preference will be taken into account in deciding your allocation."

"But not necessarily complied with?" Gerry said. "Perhaps you'd like to give me some idea of the other factors involved?"

"You have an alert mind, Clyne. I can use a man like you. But I warn you, if you do come under my command, you will have to be prepared to accept discipline."

"I'm not averse to discipline, provided I can see that it is directed towards some useful purpose," Gerry said.

"Good—then we must see what can be done. But first you will have to be examined by the medical officer." Brenner picked up a desk telephone and dialled a number. "Torrance? . . . I've a new arrival here for you to examine . . . Yes, he's already expressed a preference for military service. Do what you can, will you? Good . . . I'll send him along." He replaced the phone. "Right, Clyne. Your escort will be waiting outside. Tell him to take you along to the Medical Center."

CHAPTER SEVEN

Torrance, the medical officer, was a big, fuzzy-haired man who looked like an amiable koala bear. His heavy body slumped sacklike in a rumpled, tan-colored civilian suit, he surveyed Gerry as if he was enjoying some private joke.

"All right, Clyne—sit down, why don't you? No need to stand to attention for me."

"Thank you." Gerry obeyed without remark, but the implied reference to Brenner was not lost on him.

Torrance took a pad of foolscap-sized forms from a drawer and put it on the desk in front of him. "For a start I'm supposed to give you a complete physical examination."

"Physical—hell! I only just got through being probed and messed about by that damned Decontamination Unit."

Torrance raised one thick-fingered hand, chuckling. "All right, all right. I've heard it all before, believe me. Do you have any physical disabilities?"

"As far as I know I'm in pretty good shape," Gerry said.

"So be it," grunted Torrance. He began to make rapid notes on the form. "Bloody waste of time, all this, really. Brenner doesn't know a medulla from an anus. I doubt if he even reads half the stuff. It's my guess he just sticks it in one of those filing cabinets of his and forgets about it. But with Brenner, everything has to be done pukkah, army style, at the double, as you may have noticed. How did you get on with him, by the way?"

"You want an answer, or a polite noise," Gerry said warily.

Torrance pushed his chair back, laughing. "I take it you weren't unduly impressed."

"You could say that."

"A little man," said Torrance. "A little man who has waited all his life for an opportunity like this, and when it comes he makes a botch of it."

"You don't seem to have a very high opinion of your commanding officer," Gerry said.

"Not *my* commanding officer," Torrance said, waving one big paw derisively. "I'm the pig in the middle. Brenner, the Civil Committee, it's all the same to me—neither of them can manage without my cooperation. As for Brenner, you know what he is—a second-rate electronics technician in uniform. He makes all the right noises, but the nearest he ever got to action before this was Open Night in the Officers' Mess."

"I don't see how . . ."

"How he came to be in charge here?" Torrance supplied. "He *wasn't*. Quilter was the top man, Major Jim Quilter, but he happened to be on leave when the blowup came, and that left Brenner."

"*Major* Quilter?"

"Why sure," said Torrance. "Brenner's real rank is captain, but when he realized that he was on his own, and there was no likelihood of his being replaced, he promoted himself. Big man! I suppose he gave you his recruiting speech, by the way?"

"He suggested that I might want to volunteer for military duties," Gerry said.

"And you said?"

"Well, I didn't really commit myself. It sounds a reasonably good idea, but from what I gathered, it isn't really up to him to decide what I shall be doing."

Torrance laughed. "Maybe I'd better give you a short rundown on the political situation in here. At the time of the first attack, Brenner had forty men under his command, all of them communications specialists, rather than combat troops. The rest of our population consists of construction workers, engineers, scientists, and various clerical staff, male and female. Naturally, when the first panic was on, everybody pitched in to hold off the guerillas, and Brenner, as the resident military genius, was in command. But later, after things calmed down, a Civilian Committee was formed for administrative purposes, to organize food production and that kind of thing."

"Yes, they seem to be doing a pretty good job," Gerry said. "I saw a lot of intensive cultivation on the way here from the Decontamination Unit."

"Too good, from Brenner's point of view. There are a few of them on there, like Magruder, who could outsmart Brenner politically without even trying. He was so busy playing soldiers that he was content to leave most of the administrative work to the Committee, and before he woke up to what was going on they'd decided that a military force of a hundred men would be sufficient to maintain our perimeter and limited his recruiting accordingly. Now he has to practically get on his knees and beg for every single man he wants, which means that unless the Committee has a complete change of heart, he's never going to have a force big enough to organize a counterattack and crush the guerillas once and for all. This, when he was potentially in a position of supreme authority—when, if he'd seized the opportunity at the right time, he could have taken over the whole damned shoot and run it his way."

"A military dictatorship, you mean?"

"All right, so dictatorship is a rude word," Torrance said. "But let me put it this way—what would *you* have done, if you'd been in his position? Sure, we're all living fairly comfortably in this sector, and Brenner's limited military force is keeping the guerillas out of our hair, but it's not providing a final solution to the situation. What is really needed is a push into enemy territory—a push big enough and bloody enough to make them willing to talk terms. After all, however strong their indoctrination is, they must have doubts about the purpose of going on fighting when their homeland is irretrievably destroyed."

"Makes sense to me," Gerry said.

"Maybe, but every time Brenner tries to up his recruiting, they vote him down with some delaying argument or another—and he just has to take it."

"And you think the Council are wrong?"

"Don't *you*?" Torrance said. "We may be holding our perimeter, but unless some positive action is taken against the guerillas, they could beat us in the long run. It's like the constant dripping of water that wears away a stone. Yesterday they killed a man in a raid on one of the food stores—next week it could be half a dozen, or none . . . Brenner has his patrols out round the clock, but there's always a chance that a small group of the enemy may slip through."

Gerry nodded. "The old guerilla principle of random attacks at irregular intervals—as much psychological in its effect as physical. Yes, I see what you mean."

"You do? Good!" Torrance's round face beamed. "Then maybe if I get you allocated to the military quota you'll be able to do something about it eventually. That is, if you don't get yourself shot in the meantime."

"I'll do my best to avoid that," Gerry said.

Torrance beamed. "Fine! There's a regular meeting of the Civil Committee this evening. In the meantime Annersley will show you around and get you fixed up with some sort of accommodation."

CHAPTER EIGHT

The prisoner stood to attention, hands pressed to the side-seams of his threadbare combat uniform trousers. He was a big, fair-haired man, with a ruddy, slablike peasant face, blue eyes staring straight ahead at the flag which hung on the wall behind his commanding officer. On the prisoner's right, the regulation two paces to his rear, stood Warrant Officer Gorst, the black-bearded giant who was said to have killed at least fifteen of the enemy with his bare hands.

"Private Sikorski, it is not necessary for you to remind me that we are fighting an enemy responsible for the murder of our Motherland, nor that it is our sacred task to avenge the millions of our dead. Even after final victory is ours, it will be our duty to remember that enemy and to make sure that our descendants never forget who was responsible for the crime of the genocide against our people. But none of these facts can mitigate in any way your deliberate disobedience of my express orders, or your conduct towards this woman prisoner. You understand that for such a crime it is within my power to order you to be taken from here and summarily executed. . . ."

Captain Avram Meyer, standing to the right of the commanding officer's desk, studied the deep-furrowed, strong-featured face of Colonel Ulanov and found himself wondering once again just how much of the man's ruthless dedication to his task was the result of his natural characteristics and how much was due to the magic of the Programmers. Whatever the truth might be, Ulanov was a man of courage, and Meyer was unable to resist a feeling of sadness in the knowledge that such dedication should be devoted to a meaningless purpose; that he and the others who suffered and died here Inside should be doing so in continuation of a war which had never happened. Back in the Control Dome, looking at tapes projected onto monitor screens, and listening to Moule expounding his theories on the therapeutic value of conflict within the Controlled Environment, it had all seemed so logical, almost like some kind of chess game; but after three months within that environment, living with these people, watching their sacrifices, it had been borne in on Meyer again and again that no matter what Moule said, these were not chess pieces, or even merely experimental subjects in the laboratory sense. They were human beings, in whose fate he found himself deeply involved. Sikorski, for instance, this stupid, red-faced bumpkin, who now stood before Ulanov on a charge of attempting to rape one of the female prisoners; back on Earth he would have been able to play out his frustrations quite harmlessly with the help of a Senso-tape player, and yet here. . . .

"Prisoner, attention! About face! Quick march—left-right-left-right . . ." The roar of Warrant Officer Gorst and the crash of heavily booted feet on the wooden floor of the hut jerked Meyer from his speculations.

The door slammed behind prisoner and escort, leaving the two officers alone together; and Meyer became aware that Ulanov was regarding him, two furrows evident between the deep-set, gray eyes.

"I know what you're thinking, Meyer."

"Sir?" Although the possibility was unlikely, Meyer shifted uneasily.

"We go to great lengths to teach these men to act like animals in ways that suit our purposes—then we punish them for showing the same characteristics in other respects. Is that not so?"

"I must admit . . . ."

Ulanov's strong-featured face relaxed into a smile. "My dear Avram, you are both fortunate and unfortunate, in that you are a thinker. For men like you, war is more difficult, because you feel too much. I have perhaps more luck. I am one of the doers—the decision makers. There is an objective, and I, like a bull, put my head down and charge straight for it, not counting the possible cost."

"That is not true. You see ahead—if you didn't you would be unable to plan as well as you do," Meyer said.

Ulanov nodded his cropped head, upon which the gray hairs were steadily beginning to outnumber the black. "You may be right, Avram, but my approach is different from your own. That is why you are so valuable to me. You are, in a manner of speaking, my conscience."

God! How well you know, thought Meyer, marvelling once again at the qualities of this man who, although he could not possibly have any idea of the true nature of the forces that governed his existence, was still capable of making such penetratingly correct observations on their relationship.

"Sikorski—that trained bear," said Ulanov, relaxing

backward in his chair and lighting one of his slim brown cigars. "It is no use to talk to him of the future. All he knows are his immediate appetites. He feeds when his stomach tells him, he kills when he finds himself face to face with the enemy, and he lusts when his gonads itch. Thirty lashes will curb the itch for the time being, or at least they will make him more cautious—that is the way one must train an animal. We take no male prisoners, but the women will be necessary to us when final victory is achieved. Without them there can be no future for the united community we shall establish within the dome. Now, most of them still think of themselves as our enemies, but when the time comes they must be made to understand that they are to become the mothers of the new race—the *only* race surviving on this earth poisoned by the treachery of the war-mad, imperialist aggressors. It would have been better if they could have been of our own stock, but that, as we both know, is impossible. We shall rebuild with the materials at our disposal."

But you will never rebuild, thought Meyer. You will never be allowed to rebuild, because this conflict will go on and on forever, perpetuated by a squat, hairless man, who remains out there in the Control Dome, observing through a thousand unseen eyes and manipulating situations through Role-Players like myself. You will not even be allowed the dignity of dying. Whatever happens to your body, the grisly remnants will be taken out through a transport point and reassembled, revivified by Boehm and his surgeons. After that you will be Reprogrammed, so that the next time you may come back Inside as one of that very enemy for whom you hold such a dedicated hatred. As for this new race you speak of—has it not occurred to you that there must have been other sexual relationships between our men and the women prisoners? Gentler, more quietly conducted relationships, because men and women have need of one another, and political considerations of friend or enemy are of little consequence under such circumstances. No, not to you, with your dedication and your planning for the future; because if it had, you would realize that these affairs have produced nothing more than momentary illicit pleasure. I know that never in the history of Inside has there been such a thing as conception, nor will there be. Your goal of a future soviet peopled by the progeny of your good fighting men and the women prisoners is nothing but a dream, a sterile dream . . . Because within this environment there can be no conception, no fusion of seed, or development of foetus.

"I have decided to step up our night raids, Meyer," said Ulanov. "They are more effective than daylight operations from the morale point of view, and more economical in the matter of casualties."

The quick knife, the wire garrotte; the true horror of guerilla warfare, where murder stalks soft-footed in the darkness. Death in open battle, even the flesh-shredding horror of an exploding grenade, seemed less bestial to Meyer, but he realized that he was not really being asked for his advice—only for confirmation of a decision already made by Ulanov. Nevertheless, he spoke: "In the past that might have been true, Colonel. But Intelligence Section reports that the enemy has considerably increased the efficiency of his perimeter defenses recently, with the installation of a number of trip beams and infra-red detector units. There is also talk of a newly sown minefield in Sector 16F."

Ulanov's rugged features darkened. "Talk?" he growled. "Talk is for women and old men, Meyer. What we need —and what you're supposed to provide—are facts." He rose from behind his desk and walked across to the table which held a relief map of the dome's interior. "16F you say?"

Meyer joined him and picked up a pointer which lay at the side of the table. "16F, stretching possibly through 16G," he said, indicating an arc of territory at the southern limits of enemy country.

Ulanov topped the dark, slimly built Meyer by a good fifteen centimeters. "Possibilities are no good to me, Captain. We have, how many—four detection units? You will take a patrol of ten men tonight and map this so-called minefield—understand?"

"Would that be wise under the circumstances?" Meyer said. "It is quite possible that the whole thing is merely a rumor."

"Then we will verify *that*!" roared Ulanov.

Meyer inwardly cursed his own foolishness in questioning

Ulanov's order. By now he should have been sufficiently aware of the workings of the man's personality to recognize such a mistake before making it. One did not question, or doubt, Ulanov in this mood—one obeyed. By his error, the quiet rapport of the previous conversation was ended for the time being. His only sensible course was to get out of Ulanov's presence before more damage was done.

"Yes, Colonel. With your permission I will go right away and detail men for the patrol."

Ulanov grunted his assent, and Meyer left him brooding darkly over the map table.

Three-quarters of an hour later, having delegated final arrangements for the patrol to a sergeant, Meyer returned to his own sparsely furnished quarters. The main advantage of holding officer rank was that at least one did not have to suffer the noise and stench of a barrack room. One had—such as it was—a certain amount of privacy. Privacy, in this instance, to anticipate the grim possibilities of the night's enterprise in which he had become involved.

He checked his weapons and ammunition, and then, not feeling any inclination towards joining the other officers at their evening meal, he lay on his hard bed with the intention of getting some rest. Staring up at the bare boards of the ceiling, aware of the roiling of his gut, the oily sweat seeping from his pores, he soon realized that the prospect of any kind of relaxation was unlikely.

There was a possibility that he might die on this night patrol, a bloody, messy death, with his body torn apart by the jagged fragments of an exploded enemy mine. It made no difference to console himself with the thought that such a death would only be temporary; that cleaning up squads from the nearest transport point would pick him, or what remained of him, up and rush him back to Control for surgery and revivification. Pain and death might be only temporary, but they would nevertheless be subjectively real. On the other hand, such an event would mean that his present role Inside was concluded, that he would either be sent back to Earth, or at the very least, remain in the comfortable environment of the Control Dome for the rest of his service with the project.

55

Thinking of Ulanov and the others here Inside who faced pain and death daily without even the consoling knowledge of revivification, he found himself once again doubting his ability to carry on with this role much longer. He realized that the main source of his difficulty was an overactive imagination, but there was little he could do about that, apart from drugging himself into insensibility, and that was no real solution. The question was, where did imagination end, and cowardice begin? Ulanov and the others were strengthened by their dedication and sense of purpose, but he too had a purpose. The difficulty lay in the fact that over the past few weeks his belief in the validity of that purpose was being gradually eroded by a feeling of futility and isolation.

But he was not alone—*ever*. As if to remind him of this fact, the microtransceiver implanted in the bone behind his left ear emitted its tiny *beep*.

"Avram, are you all right?" The quality of the voice, remarkably faithful despite the miniscule nature of the loud-speaker, was clearly that of Laura Frayne.

"Me? I'm just fine," he replied.

"Don't try to con me, Avram."

He found himself smiling, visualizing the fine-boned, beautifully formed features of the woman who sat in the communications center back at Control.

"Would I do that to you, mother dear?"

She swore, with delicately precise profanity. "You're worrying about this night patrol, aren't you?"

It was no surprise to him that she knew about the mission. Even if she had not watched and listened to the conversation between himself and Ulanov personally, Monitor Section would have sent her a taped extract, considering it an event of some importance.

"You know goddamned well I am!"

"Easy, Avram, easy . . ." she said.

The knowledge that she was trying to soothe him only served to increase his frustration. "There's no use kidding ourselves, Laura—I've *had* this role. I want out—OUT —out!"

"You don't really mean that, Avram." Her voice was quiet, patient.

56

Lying on the hard bed shaking his head from side to side, he grimaced. "Listen to me, Laura, for God's sake listen! I don't believe in what I'm doing any more. Inside—the whole thing, is a waste, a senseless waste. Can you imagine what it's like to live with these people from day to day, knowing them, feeling empathy for them, and having to watch them suffer needlessly?"

"I don't have to imagine," she replied, her voice hardening. "I've *been* there. Each time we get a revivification case in, I have a copy tape made before reprogramming. I know how they suffer, how they die . . . I've done it with them, men, women . . . Do you know what it's like to lie dying, face down in the dirt, with a hole in your chest big enough to stick a fist through, blood bubbling from smashed lungs? Do you know what it feels like, that moment when the jet from a flame-thrower hits you and the skin of your body begins to stretch and. . . ."

She was telling him the truth, he had no doubt of that. This tall, handsome woman with the heart of a lioness would not spare herself any experience that was capable of increasing her understanding of the work she had to do, nor would she indulge in the kind of self-pity that plagued himself. He knew the truth, and it shamed him, but still. . . .

"Laura, I just can't take it any more, I've lost the meaning, if there ever was one. All I see is suffering and death of a kind that no reasons can justify." Avram Meyer clamped his clenched fists to aching temples, moaning his agony to the empty room.

"I know, Avram, I know." Laura's voice was gentle again. "But there is hope, new hope, I promise you."

"How can there be hope, while this goes on?"

"It may not go on for much longer."

The words pierced the isolating shell of his despair. "You mean there's to be a change? Moule has decided to end all this at last?"

"Not quite that, but a move has been made, a new factor introduced."

"What? Tell me what, for God's sake, Laura!"

"I can't explain more at this stage. You must trust me, Avram."

"Trust!"

"Later I shall be able to tell you more, for now that will have to be all. But when the time comes, we shall have need of you. There will be an important part for you to play. Avram, go on for just a while longer. I promise you it will end, and that you will help in its ending, in the building of a new hope."

"Why are you telling me this? Is the whole thing just so much pap to humor me?"

"No, Avram—it is the truth, all of the truth that I dare tell you at this time. Be patient, and hold on just a while longer. And take care of yourself."

Beep. The contact was broken, and Avram Meyer lay, once more alone on his hard bed, knowing that for her, this woman in whom he trusted and believed, he would go on. He would go on for as long as he could, because even if what she had told him was all lies, a man had to believe in *something*.

CHAPTER NINE

Davidson had arranged to meet Laura Frayne at 20:30 in the Saturn Bar because he expected that by that time the early evening drinkers would be gone and they would have the place more or less to themselves. Instead, when he arrived he found a laughing, chattering crowd bunched in between the counter and the main entrance like a flock of chickens round a load of spilled corn. He elbowed his way through the crush of bodies, a fixed grin on his face as he returned several alcoholically enthusiastic greetings from people who would not normally have bothered to acknowledge his presence.

Laura was sitting at a table at the far end of the long, low room, with two drinks in front of her. She pointed to one. "I thought I'd save you the job of fighting your way up to the counter."

"Thanks," he said, looking back towards the crowd. "Bird-brained idiots! What is it, anyway—some kind of celebration?"

When he turned back to face her she was shaking her honey-blonde hair from side to side, smiling. "Really, Michael, sometimes I wonder if you take any notice at all of what's going on around you."

Her condescension irritated him doubly because of his immediate response to her lithe, desirable body. "So what's that supposed to mean?" he demanded.

"Surely you hadn't forgotten that the *Orion* was due in tonight," she said.

As if cued in by her remark, the bar's wall screens, which had been showing synaesthetic abstracts attuned to the neo-jazz that was being piped through the sound system, dissolved into blankness. The noise from the crowd of drinkers hushed suddenly as the blankness was replaced a moment later by the well-known smile of Earl Madison, utility man announcer/newscaster to the Control Dome's video station.

"Well, hello there, all you Earth-watching time-servers!" jollied Madison's ripe bourbon baritone. "At this point we interrupt our scheduled programs to bring you a direct coverage of the approach and touch-down of the good ship *Orion*. First of all, a few words with Captain Checkman, who you all . . ."

Davidson stared contemptuously at the silent, screen-watching crowd. "Look at that! Two minutes ago they were all yelling their heads off, and now they're listening to this drivel they've heard at least a dozen times before as if their lives depended on it."

"Well they do, in a way, don't they?" Laura said quietly. "The safe arrival of the *Orion* is an event of some importance."

"I'm not denying that. But I don't see any point in ramming the whole boring sequence down our throats every month. This business of the big celebration each time she arrives reminds me of some primitive cargo cult. I know we depend to a large extent on the supplies *Orion* brings in, but what's so special about it every time?"

"You're in a minority."

"That's not unusual," he said.

"Perhaps you never get tired of living in this overturned goldfish bowl," Laura said. "But I know that it does me

59

good, for one, to look at a screen and think to myself that Earth is only as far away as that ship.''

"You mean you're homesick?"

"Call it that, if you like—or a need for reassurance. It gives me a feeling of keeping in touch," she said, looking at the nearest screen. "And then there's the prospect of letters and tapes. Don't you correspond with anybody back there?"

"Like who, for instance? The girl next door? A little old silvery-haired mother?" Davidson said bitterly. "I'll tell you something. The only girl I might like to correspond with is right here on Mars, and she doesn't want to know. As for my mother, she takes a course of DNA rejuvenation therapy twice a year, and in between she's usually pretty busy getting herself married or divorced. In any case, she made it clear the last time she did send me a tape that she found the necessity of having to admit to the existence of a thirty-year-old son a social embarrassment.''

"Poor Mike!" Laura's hand moved towards his in an impulsive gesture of sympathy.

He withdrew from the touch, feeling an inward flaring resentment at her expression of pity. Sometimes it seemed to him that she enjoyed torturing him in that way, arousing him by her presence, her apparent availability. Perhaps it was partly because of this that he found himself desiring her, and at the same time feeling a resentment against her that was close to hatred.

"I think I'd better go," he said. "I had intended to talk to you about the present situation Inside, but this doesn't seem to be the time.''

"Of course it's the time," she said. The screens were showing a long shot of the approaching ship, but she turned and looked directly at him. "You're quite right, Michael —one touchdown is much like another. Interesting though, from the Psyche point of view—" she glanced at the silent screen watchers "—I sometimes think that there's more than an element of sympathetic magic in this vigil; that they're watching the landing, each of them consciously contributing his or her little push of goodwill in an attempt to make sure that everything goes well. Whatever is the truth, they're each

60

of them fully absorbed in what's going on—so we're as alone as we could be anywhere.''

Davidson accepted her suggestion. "Have you seen any monitor tapes on Clyne?'' he asked.

She nodded. "You did a good job there—almost too good.''

"Too good?'' There was something about her expression that he could not interpret—in some vague manner she seemed ill-at-ease.

"Yes, I've been having queries on the cooperation bit. The way Torrance has it, Clyne won't need much help from him. He's quite capable of taking over through his own efforts, and he's well on the road towards doing so. He started out by talking the Civil Committee into allocating him for military duty, and in the last three weeks, through a number of successful operations, he's established himself as a natural leader in the field. Apparently the men like him, because he's always up there in the front in action, and Brenner likes him, because he's taking some of the weight off his back.''

"That's the way I heard it,'' Davidson said. "Somehow he's managed to gain the trust of both sides—the civil and the military—which is a good beginning. If I could only find a suitable subject for programming his equivalent in the Southern Sector, we'd really be in business.''

"No prospect of anything yet?''

Davidson shrugged. "I could get the right man tomorrow—or it might take six months. How can you tell?''

"In that case, it looks as though I shall have to do something about Avram Meyer. I had hoped to hold him in there until the new subject was established, but if it's going to be a long wait, I may have to take him out.''

"Why? What's the trouble?''

"One of the main difficulties is that he's *too* good—he's always been hypersensitive, but now he's developing an alarming degree of involvement with Ulanov and the group aims of the Southern Sector,'' Laura said. "I'm less and less able to predict his reactions in stress situations, and that can be dangerous in a Role-Player.''

"But that's stupid! How can he become so involved when he knows the whole thing is just an artificially created dramatic situation?"

"How can a mind accept two 'realities'?" Laura countered. "For that matter—what is *reality*?"

He looked away, trying to hide the hunger in his eyes. He wanted to say: "Reality is you and me, it's the longing my body has for you, the need I have for you alone." But instead he forced a harsh laugh and said: "Don't you go philosophical on me, Laura—that I can't take. The point is, right now we don't want any changes Inside other than those that fit in with our plans. How much have you told Meyer so far?"

"Very little—only that there is going to be a change, and that there would be a part for him to play in that change."

"And his reaction?"

"He wanted to know more, but I stalled him," Laura said. "I tell you one thing, Michael—we're going to have trouble with him over the replacement of Ulanov. He looks on the man as some kind of hero figure."

"But it's all false," Davidson said. "Ulanov is just a slob who was programmed with this gallant guerilla leader stuff. He's a puppet, playing out the dramatic role laid down for him."

"From *our* point of view, possibly," Laura said. "But we're not in there, involved in the same way that Avram Meyer is."

"He's really that bad?" Davidson frowned. "Hell! If I only knew for sure that it would be another month or so before a suitable second subject came up I'd suggest you take Meyer out from Inside right away. But the right man could turn up tomorrow, and then the presence of a Role-Player in Meyer's precise situation would be essential."

Laura nodded her understanding. "I'll hold him in there for the time being, but if he shows signs of deteriorating any further, then I shall have to pull him out and trust to luck."

CHAPTER TEN

"Ah, Michael—good of you to come," Moule said. "Please sit down."

Davidson lowered himself into a chair, at the same time trying to read the expression on the other's hypnotically ugly features. The call to report to the Director's office had come early on the morning following his conversation with Laura in the Saturn Bar. There had been no point in questioning the secretary who had delivered the message, so he had abandoned the routine work on which he was occupied and hurried straight over to the administration building.

Moule's elephantine body shifted forward slightly as he leaned over the desk, his pale amber eyes looking deep into those of his subordinate. "Tell me, Michael—are you happy here?"

"Happy?" The odd nature of the question increased Davidson's feeling of unease.

"Let me put it another way," Moule said gently. "Do you find your work as a Programmer an excessive strain at times?"

Davidson searched his mind for a suitable answer, unwilling to commit himself until he knew the purpose of this interview. "I don't suppose there's any worthwhile job that is without its moments of stress or of tedium. Naturally the work is demanding. . ."

"Perhaps you could be more specific?"

"That would be easier if I knew just what we were talking about," Davidson said, his unease being gradually replaced by impatience.

"All right, let me put it in another way," Moule said, placing his huge, pale hands downwards on the desk in front of him. "As you know, the field of Programming is one in which I myself have worked extensively in the past, so I understand the problems you face. If he is to perform his work well, a Programmer must be capable of a high degree of empathy with each subject he handles, and only a person of high sensitivity can have such a capability. Add to this the fact that, despite all artificial aids, only another human mind is capable of tailoring a program to the needs and drives of a specific human personality; the fact that however methodical we may try to be, we have not yet succeeded in devising a method of computerizing the process, and we begin to get some measure of the kind of responsibility placed on the mind of a Programmer. He is dealing all the time with dangerously explosive intangibles, abstract concepts, attitudes, passions, forming and reforming such materials in his own mind, and transferring them to the mind of the subject with the aid of the Programming Induction Unit. This being so, it is necessary that a great deal of the work of a Programmer is to a large degree intuitive, a process which can only find its true analogy in the act of artistic creation.''

''Yes, I think I would agree with you there,'' Davidson said.

''This being so,'' Moule continued, ''the Programmer is constantly trying to balance himself between the pole of scientific detachment on the one hand and that of empathy and understanding on the other. Too much rational calculation on his part, and he may be in danger of forcing a program on the subject which could render him little more than a puppet; whereas should he allow himself to become too emotionally involved, then he may place his own mind in danger. I have warned you in the past that you are liable to err on the side of overinvolvement. It seems to me that this may have happened in the case of this man Clyne.''

Davidson suppressed a start of alarm at the mention of the name. ''I was dealing with a very strong paranoid personality pattern, which seemed to me to demand the kind of manipulation I afforded it. You yourself scanned some extracts from the background I found it necessary to provide.''

''And my reactions were, if you remember, not entirely approving,'' Moule said. ''However, that is not important at the moment. I am more concerned with your own personal welfare.''

Still trying to guess at the ultimate purpose of this interview, Davidson remained silent as the director turned his attention to a green file which lay on the desk in front of him.

"Tell me, Michael," he said, without looking up, "why did you volunteer for the position of Programmer in the first instance?"

Why? Davidson paused deliberately, searching among the alternatives that came into his mind. He sensed that it was somehow important that he should find the right answer—if there was one.

"I think possibly because I felt that in such work I could be of help to people who needed me, and at the same time have the opportunity of expressing my own individuality," he replied, at length.

Moule looked up, a trace of humor apparent in his pale eyes. "Not an easy combination, would you say? To help —and yet at the same time to dominate."

"I said nothing about domination," Davidson replied quickly, incensed by what seemed to him a deliberate misinterpretation of his motives.

"Please don't be offended," Moule said, calmly. "I am not accusing you of any crime. The urge to dominate is a perfectly natural human drive. But yours, as we have already established, must be a special case; firstly, because you are a Programmer, and secondly, because you are clearly not in agreement with the policy I have followed with regard to the dramatic situation Inside."

"I have never attempted to conceal my misgivings about that policy," Davidson said sharply. "But I believe that I have always done my work to the best of my ability."

"That may well be so," Moule said. "But it should be obvious that your talent for empathizing with your subjects, combined with this admitted opposition to my policy, must place you on a constant knife edge of tension, producing a potentially dangerous conflict situation which could have serious effects on your own personality pattern. I want you to understand that this is merely an off-the-cuff diagnosis, an attempt to explain the changes in your Psyche Profile which showed up in the latest check, but I suspect that deep-probing will provide confirmation."

Davidson was alert now, his thin body quivering with

tension. "Now just a minute, even if a slight instability has shown up in my Profile, there are no legal, psycho/social grounds on which I could be forced to accept deep-probing."

"I don't think any mention was made of force, was it?" Moule said mildly. "But in view of the special nature of your work, I would be failing in my duty if I allowed the matter to remain uninvestigated. There may be no real reason for alarm—but on the other hand, these new readings may indicate the growth of a potentially dangerous psychosis on a deeper level."

Davidson was aware of an increasing sense of helplessness as he felt the trap closing about him. Deep-probing was a technique he himself used as a matter of routine in his work as a Programmer, but if he allowed such an examination to be made of his own mind, the manner in which he had modified Clyne's Programming, and the motives that lay behind his actions would be exposed. Once such information was placed in the hands of Moule, the plan involving Clyne would be completely wrecked. The situation was made even worse by his realization that Agostino, whose department was responsible for the preparation of the Profile report, could not fail to be aware of its possible consequences.

"And if I refuse to accept deep-probing?" he said.

"In such an event, I'm afraid that I should be forced to rule that you are no longer capable of carrying out your duties as a Programmer," Moule said, his face stonily impassive.

"I would be reallocated to another department?"

Moule shook his bald head slowly. "No, in a case like yours such a course of action would be unwise. Your personality pattern is such that you would not be likely to settle quietly into a subordinate role in some other type of work. In your present condition you would no longer be of use to the project, in fact the indications are that you could be a positive danger to its continuance. Under the circumstances I'm afraid you leave me no alternative but to order your return to Earth."

"But my contract!"

"Will be terminated on grounds of unfitness for duty, and you will be adequately compensated," Moule said. "I shall arrange with Captain Checkman for you to return to Earth on the *Orion* when she leaves tomorrow night. In the meantime I suggest that you collect your belongings and make your farewells.''

''But you can't send me back just like that!'' protested Davidson.

''The choice was your own, Davidson,'' said the Director. ''There might have been some hope if you had been prepared to accept deep-probing. As it is, I must do what I consider best for the welfare of the project. And now, if you will excuse me. . . .''

Stunned by the sudden destruction of his plans for the future, Davidson walked slowly out of Moule's office.

CHAPTER ELEVEN

Laura Frayne's first reaction when Michael Davidson burst into her Section and demanded to speak to her alone had been one of annoyance, but when he explained the reason for his urgency the mood soon passed.

''So Moule wins in the end, after all,'' she said sadly. It was obvious to her that the plan for which they had both been working would never succeed now. Boehm, Hofer and the others—she herself, for that matter—had come to depend on Davidson's leadership in this thing. Without his driving force there was little possibility that the matter would be pressed further, and the situation Inside would go on indefinitely on the lines laid down by Moule. The suffering and the killing would continue, and she would have to watch it, powerless to make any change.

''Not if we act *now*,'' Davidson said.

She frowned. ''But how can we? Surely we're not ready . . . You're still waiting for an opportunity of establishing a new leader in the Southern Sector—and in the north Clyne hasn't taken over yet.''

Davidson moved edgily about the room as he talked, seemingly unable to remain in one place for more than a few seconds at a time. ''Clyne has the potential backing. If

Brenner were to be removed, his takeover of command would be almost automatic.''

''Removed?''

He came closer to her, and she could see the twitching of the small muscles beneath the pale skin of his face. ''Laura, do you believe in the need for a change Inside? You've not just been *talking* about this thing?''

''Of course I believe,'' she said. ''But surely to make a half-hearted unsuccessful attempt would be worse than to do nothing at all? And I just don't see how it is possible to do anything really effective in the thirty-six hours that remain before *Orion* leaves for Earth.''

''I am not talking about an *unsuccessful* attempt,'' Davidson's voice crackled with tension. ''What we have to do can be done in a different, quicker way than originally planned. In fact, the very speed with which it is carried out will be a positive advantage, making it less likely that Moule will have the slightest idea what is going on until we've succeeded. This can be done, I tell you—but only if we act boldly and swiftly. The first move must be made by you. I want you to call Torrance and tell him that Brenner is to die from an apparent coronary.''

''Kill Brenner?'' She recoiled at the thought of such cold-blooded execution.

Davidson gestured impatiently. ''He will be brought back here and revivified as a matter of course. The main point is that he should be removed from Inside.''

''I'm not sure that Torrance would accept such an order from me,'' Laura said.

''Not from you—from *Moule*,'' Davidson said. ''You have already told him that the Director intends Clyne to take over control of the Northern Sector eventually. It shouldn't be too difficult to convince him that Moule has decided to step up the natural progression of events by a small piece of additional manipulation. After all, what are Role-Players in there for but this kind of thing?''

Laura found the logic of the move obscure. ''All right, supposing I do persuade Torrance to accept such an order, I still don't see just how the installation of a new leader in the north is likely to bring about the results we want. If anything,

I would have thought that a takeover by Clyne would make matters worse, because it seems to me likely that one of his first moves would be to step up military operations in an effort to gain a decisive victory over the guerillas."

"Possibly, if he were allowed to remain in his present state of ignorance," Davidson said. "But you're forgetting that I have already prepared for such a situation in his original Programming. Once he has taken over, I shall reactivate the suppressed memory patterns in his mind. He will then be prepared to accept my guidance in bringing an end to the futile conflict Inside."

"It seems to me that you may be oversimplifying, Michael," Laura said. "The monitor tapes I've seen on Clyne indicate to me, at least, that he is more inclined to lead than to follow. I can hardly imagine him meekly accepting your orders, even when he does know the truth about the controlled environment."

"You've seen some tapes on Clyne?" Davidson said sharply.

"Naturally. That is a necessary part of my work, especially since he has been closely associated with Torrance." This was only part of the truth. In fact, Laura had found herself so fascinated by Clyne that she had requested additional material from Monitor Section. The man seemed to be possessed of an aggressive maleness, which combined with undoubted intelligence in a manner that she found herself unable, or unwilling to resist. Watching him on her playback screen she had sometimes found herself thinking that perhaps with such a man she would be able to escape the disastrous pattern which had dominated her male/female relationships for so long; but Michael Davidson was the last person to whom she would confide such thoughts. Thinking it wiser at the present time to change the direction of the discussion, she said: "All right, supposing you are able to come to some kind of working arrangement with Clyne when he knows the truth about Inside, your original plan was based on the achievement of an early truce between north and south, to be agreed between the two leaders Programmed by yourself. In the event, there will only be one such leader, Clyne. Ulanov, on the other hand, is an uncompromising, near-fanatic, who would rather die than even consider the possibility of such a truce."

"That is his attitude at the moment," agreed Davidson. "But attitudes can be changed, as you know very well."

"With the aid of the equipment at your disposal in the Programming Section, possibly," Laura said. "But Ulanov is Inside. It would be impossible to remove him from the environment and bring him back here for Reprogramming in the time you have—even if you could do so without Moule intervening."

"Then the job will have to be done Inside," Davidson said. "I have already arranged with Jack Hofer for the loan of his modified Senso-tape player."

Laura shuddered inwardly as she considered the implications of what Davidson had said. It was an open secret amongst the senior members of the Control staff that Jack Hofer, a brilliant electronics engineer, was also a tape-worm. Senso-tape players as normally marketed were fairly harmless, entertaining toys, inducing ghost sensory impressions in a blurry kind of way, their effectiveness depending a great deal on the quality of the subject's suspension of disbelief and his innate imaginative powers. Hofer's Senso-taper was something else again. It dug its hooks in deep from the first moment you put on the induction cap, reproducing ordinary, easily available library tapes with a fidelity that was normally lost in the fuzz of a commercial player. Hofer's modifications were not unique, in the sense that nobody had ever thought of them before. Commercial players could have been made to produce such results, but under Socio-Psyche Department orders they were deliberately made to a lower specification, because continual overstimulation by such a machine was capable of producing a permanent retreat from reality in some subjects, leaving them in a catatonic trance state, locked in an infinitely repeating dream, completely unaware of the world outside themselves.

Most of the tape-worms back on Earth were amateurs, trying to boost commercial players with secondhand parts bought from shady dealers at fancy prices, working in the dark most of the time, with no circuit diagrams, and experimenting by trial and error—errors whose results were frequently disastrous to their own sanity. Hofer, on the other hand, was a professional, an electronics specialist who spent a great deal of his working life servicing the masses of equipment used in the Programming Section, and the Programming Induction Units were, after all, little more than hyperpowered, selectively controlled Senso-tape players. This being so, Hofer had no need to rely on faulty second-hand components. He could merely put in an indent to stores for any item he wanted, in the pretence that it was needed as a replacement in connection with servicing the Induction Units.

"And the tape for this operation?" Laura asked.

"I still have access to the Programming Section," said Davidson. "It will entail a couple of hours' work, at the most, to prepare a suitable program from stock library material."

"But the permanent effects on Ulanov . . ."

Davidson smiled thinly. "You worry too much, Laura. Sure the feeding in of such a tape in this way will give his orientation quite a jolt, but his Ego-integrity is strong enough to stand up to a bit of punishment. I don't foresee any difficulty, once we've got him hooked in."

"We?"

"Your little friend Avram Meyer, and I," Davidson said.

"You're expecting Avram to help you in this?"

"Why naturally," Davidson said. "This is his big chance to do something about those heart-searchings of his at last."

"But you don't understand," Laura protested. "Avram is completely devoted to Ulanov—he idealizes the man. I doubt if he would cooperate in something like this if he realized the potential danger to Ulanov."

"Then we won't make a point of telling him, will we?" Davidson said. "Now, I must go and prepare that tape, and see some of the others. I'll be back to check with you early this afternoon, all right?"

Laura sat for a long time after he had gone, considering the possibilities of the situation. Perhaps she was just an armchair revolutionary, a talker, after all. Now that the wheels of the machine had been set in motion she was beginning to have serious misgivings. Davidson was right in principle, and she had backed him in the past—but now there was a dangerous euphoria in him, a lack of consideration of the possible cost of his efforts in terms of the suffering of others. Maybe Michael had always been that way, but she had been blinded by her own idealism. Impatient with herself, she dismissed the misgivings. The time for self-examination was past—now she had to act. She walked across to the communications console.

Torrance was an oldtimer, who had already been established Inside long before Laura had taken over her post as Section Controller, and although he never directly reminded her of this fact there was no doubt in her mind that consciousness of his seniority played a large part in both their attitudes towards each other. Not that he was envious of her position. She had no doubts on that score. Torrance was not the type of man to be tied down to an administrative desk, making reports to the Director, bearing with everybody's gripes, and generally wet-nursing the assorted Role-Players who came and went from time to time within the controlled environment. Torrance, as he had put it himself on one of his infrequent visits to the Control Dome, was an "Inside" man, with a mind so compartmented that he was capable of accepting without reservation the reality of what went on within the environment, whilst at the same time being aware of his true function and his relationship to the "real" world of the Control Dome.

She had met him in person only three times; a great, shaggy bear of a man, whose sagging, scruffy clothes seemed totally out of place in the aseptic, robot-cleaned corridors of the Control Dome. Each time he had treated her with a kind of Old World courtesy which she rather enjoyed, even while she wondered about the possible hint of mockery that lay behind his bulging brown eyes. This being so, she did not share Davidson's certainty that he would accept the orders she was about to give him without question. She was grateful for the fact that, although she could see him on the monitor screen, his only sensory contact with her was through the sound of her voice, relayed through the micro-speaker implanted in his skull.

Her misgivings proved to have some foundation. After listening to what she had to say, he replied: "I tell you frankly, Laura, I'm not happy about this Clyne business at all. I've been carrying out a policy of cooperation with him in accordance with your orders, but the more I see of him, the more I think that the Director may have miscalculated. As a leader, Brenner has just the right level of ineffectiveness to maintain the *status quo*. If Clyne takes over, God knows what may happen. By the way, who programmed him?"

"Davidson."

"Well, in my opinion he went too far," grumbled Torrance. "Have you seen any monitor shots of this man in action?"

Laura had, but realizing that the question was purely rhetorical, she remained silent as Torrance continued: "I just can't see the reason for rushing into this thing. Policy of cooperation! Clyne didn't need me, or anybody else, to help him—you realize that? And as for clearing the road for him, by getting rid of Brenner, is concerned, where's the need? He's already got 90 percent of the military and civilian sections of the northern community behind him, and he'll take over when it suits him, make no mistake about that. Clyne is a one-man planet buster, with a paranoid streak a mile wide and a line of talk good enough to charm his way out of any situation."

"I think you're overestimating Clyne," Laura said, despite the fact that her own assessment was very similar.

"Overestimating be damned!" exploded Torrance. "I've watched this man in action and listened to him. Once he takes over, he'll launch an extermination drive against the south, and he'll get all the support he needs from this community to do it. After that, I honestly think that Inside won't hold him—he's too big to accept its limitations. He's already hinted that once the war is over, he'd like to send an exploratory party outside the dome."

"You worry too much, Bob," said Laura. "It will be a long time before he's ready to tackle anything of that nature."

"So *you* say, but I'm not so sure." Torrance refused to be placated. "He thinks big, and he moves fast. If things ever

73

were allowed to get to that stage, and he sent such an expedition out, what do you imagine would happen to the conditional reality of this entire environment?''

Seen from Torrance's point of view, the possibility of the Insiders breaking out and discovering that instead of living under a protective dome on a devastated Earth, they were in fact some sixty million kilometers away on another planet, was a potentially disastrous one which, if it did nothing else, would destroy the careful work of years. And she knew that it would be completely hopeless at this stage to attempt to convert him to Michael Davidson's belief that such a step would be less harmful in the long run than the continuation of the parade of human suffering which seemed doomed to go on and on Inside under the present set-up. Clyne's real function was as an instrument to stabilize the social situation Inside, and once this goal was achieved, even an individuality such as his could be curbed by the resources available to the workers in the Control Dome.

"Bob! Now you know that's complete fantasy," she chided, trying to inject a note of playfulness into her voice.

"Like hell it's fantasy!" roared Torrance. "You're a good girl, Laura, but *I* know about what goes on in here."

"Nobody's denying that, Bob—but these are the Director's orders."

"In that case maybe I'm wasting my time talking to you," Torrance said." Look, why don't you put me through to Moule direct, and let me straighten him out on a few things?"

"I'm sorry, you know I can't do that," said Laura, a twinge of panic sharpening her voice. "The Director is very busy just now, and in any case, all reports have to go through the proper channels, as you know. I'll send him a complete recording of our conversation, then if he wants to get in touch with you . . .''

"Channels! Reports!" shouted Torrance. "All right, do it your way, but make sure he gets that recording."

"And the instructions?" Laura hardly dared bring the subject up, but the urgency of the situation left her no alternative.

"All right, I'll fix Brenner with a believable coronary. But I want action—a definite prognosis on the new dramatic pattern. And tell the Director that if there's been a change in policy, I think my rank entitles me to full information."

Laura allowed herself a silent sigh of relief. "You're sure you want all that left in your report? I mean, the Director isn't going to like . . ."

"You just send him the recording, and let me worry about that, little girl," Torrance said.

"Yes, Bob. Goodbye for now." Laura broke contact, then pressed a button on the console and watched as the tape sped quietly past the erase head. When all trace of the conversation with Torrance had been obliterated, she put through another call to Monitor Section and asked for a camera fix on Avram Meyer, in the Southern Sector.

CHAPTER TWELVE

Michael Davidson had decided long ago that his most reliable allies were Jack Hofer and Laura. This was fortunate in a sense, because it was on these two in particular that his mission depended. Hofer, because in addition to supplying the modified Senso-taper which was to be used in the Reprogramming of Ulanov, the Electronics Section head was the only person in Control capable of arranging and maintaining the communications blackout which was essential for Davidson's success, in the early stages at least. Laura, because her radio link with the Role-Players and himself would remain unaffected by Hofer's blackout, and she would provide him with the information about the situation Inside which would enable him to coordinate his plan.

As far as the other three were concerned, Boehm, Agostino and Pelissier, they had no immediate part to play in matters that went on within the controlled environment, but they would nevertheless be important, later. The successful manipulation of the dramatic situation Inside was only the first stage of the plan. Even when this was completed, and the changed situation stabilized, Moule would still remain —nominally, at least—Director of the Project. He and his

75

methods were unpopular, but there were sure to be a certain number of people within the Control Dome who for one reason or another remained loyal to Moule and might in one way or another resist any attempt to depose him. Davidson did not visualize any outbreaks of violence within the Control Dome, but rather a bloodless coup. This depended on a tacit assumption that the natural loyalty of most of the Control staff was to their respective Section Heads, rather than the Director. Naturally it would have been impossible, even if there had been time, to take all these people into his confidence before beginning action on the plan—he had to rely on the assumption that, once presented with the *fait accompli* of success, and informed of the complicity of their Section Heads, the popular majority would support the change.

Just how willing that complicity might be in the case of Agostino was a matter which had exercised Davidson's mind ever since that morning when he received news of his unfavorable stability profile from Moule. As he went about the business of preparing the programming tape for Ulanov, Davidson found himself wondering how he was going to tackle the matter of Agostino. No doubt it would have been naive to expect the Psyche deliberately to falsify his report, on the other hand, he must have had some idea what effect the new profile-rating might have on Davidson's future. Of course, this was assuming that the new profile was in fact a true one—Davidson was brought up with a jerk. Agostino had been less than enthusiastic about the plan at the last meeting of the group. Was it possible that there had, after all, been falsification in the preparation of the Psyche Profile —but falsification of another kind?

Say, for instance, that Agostino's lukewarm feelings had crystallized since that last meeting into definite opposition towards the plan, but that he had been unwilling to commit himself by going directly to Moule and exposing the activities of the group. Instead, realizing that the materialization of the plan into action depended mainly on Davidson, might it not be that he had taken the opportunity presented by the routine profile check to ensure that Davidson was declared unfit for further service on the project? Such manipulation would be a simple matter for someone in Agostino's position—he would know just which aspects of the profile to change, which instabilities to accentuate, in order to make Moule's decision a foregone conclusion. And, knowing Davidson's attitude towards deep-probing, he would be able to assume quite safely that he would not submit to any examination which might contradict the lies contained in a falsified Psyche Profile.

Distracted by the possibility of Agostino's treachery, he abandoned his work temporarily and paced the room in agitation. Now that he considered the matter, he found it difficult to imagine why he had not understood the true situation earlier—especially as he had been uneasy about Agostino for some time. But what to do—now—at this crucial stage? He could certainly not surrender to the trembling rage which urged him to rush along to Psyche Section and smear the fat Italian over his own office walls. Violence might provide a certain momentary satisfaction, but it would solve nothing, and most certainly it would jeopardize the continuation of his mission.

The sensible thing would be to hold his tongue and his temper, to conceal his discovery of the truth for the time being, and treat Agostino as a loyal ally. There were other things to be said in favor of such an exercise in control; for one, the obvious fact that after the success of the plan, and the deposing of Moule, he would be in a much stronger position to handle Agostino in any way he wished. His lean face broke into a smile as the possibilities of the situation became more apparent to him. Yes, he would wait, continuing to use Agostino for as long as it suited him. Revenge would be all the sweeter for its postponement, an added savor to victory. He turned back to the editing console and recommenced work on the Ulanov tape.

It was the middle of the afternoon when he returned to Laura Frayne's section. The heady elation he felt at the prospect of success did not blind him to the tensions apparent in her face as she greeted him.

"Is there something wrong?" he asked. "Did you have any difficulty with Torrance?"

77

"He grumbled a bit—even wanted to talk to Moule direct, but in the end he agreed to do as he was told."

"Good! Then there's nothing to worry about," Davidson said, still sensing an unexpected lack of enthusiasm in her. "Then I can leave events in the Northern Sector to take their natural course, and concentrate for the time being on the matter of Reprogramming Ulanov."

"You've prepared the tape?"

"Naturally. I shall go into the Southern Sector just after nightfall. I want you to arrange with Meyer to meet me at the underground exit point."

Laura frowned. "I talked with Avram Meyer, as well as with Torrance. I'm not happy about the way he may take this."

"Not happy? I don't understand," Davidson said. "His part in this will be very undemanding. All he has to do is arrange for me to get into Ulanov's private quarters without being intercepted by the guards, and after that to keep them off my back while I'm feeding the tape into him. Look, why don't you get him again, and let me explain?"

"No . . . I don't think that would be a very good idea," Laura said.

Davidson's impatience flared into sudden anger. "Now what the hell's that supposed to mean?" he demanded. "I know Meyer has always been a special pet of yours, but this is carrying things too far. There's no danger, if he just does as he's told. The whole thing is a perfectly simple operation of a kind that should be routine for any Role-Player."

"I disagree," Laura said firmly. "Avram Meyer has been in a condition of increasing stress for some time, as I have already explained to you. Add to this his personal involvement with Ulanov, and you have a potentially dangerous situation. It might be different if he had been prepared earlier by a full knowledge of the plan, but to push him in at the deep end like this could have serious consequences."

"So what do you suggest we do—drop the whole thing in order to spare Meyer's feelings? For God's sake be realistic, Laura. You know as well as I do that if we don't act now, within the next few hours, there just won't be another opportunity, and I shall go back to Earth on the *Orion*."

78

"I'm not suggesting any such thing," she said, facing him boldly. "I fully realize the urgency of Reprogramming Ulanov. The operation will have to be tackled in a different way, that's all."

"All right, then—you tell me," Davidson said. "What's the alternative?"

"Let *me* go Inside and handle the Reprogramming of Ulanov," she said. "It's the obvious thing. Meyer will accept the situation much better if I explain it to him, and he is used to working with me."

He regarded her steadily. What she was saying made sense, from the practical point of view, but it introduced an additional hazard of which only he was aware. There was no doubt that Laura was capable of carrying out the task of Reprogramming Ulanov just as well as himself, neither was there any denying the fact that she would be more likely to obtain the full cooperation of Meyer. But the introduction of Laura into the Inside environment brought with it the possibility of a meeting between herself and Clyne, and this was something which he had been determined to avoid. Because of his Programming, Clyne was possessed of a built-in affinity for Kay, who had been created in Laura's image—and any meeting with Laura might well produce a new, unpredictable emotional situation at a time when the predictability of Clyne's responses was essential. Even though it seemed highly unlikely that Laura would respond positively to any such feelings on the part of Clyne—after all, a woman of her intelligence would hardly be attracted by such a crude brute—it was a situation which he would rather not put to the test, at this time in particular.

"Apart from anything else, surely my going Inside would make your own position easier?" Laura said. "After all, you can't be in two places at once—and you may have quite enough to do handling Clyne, not to mention any possible difficulties with Torrance."

He still hesitated. "But what about communications? I had relied on your being here, in case of any emergency."

"If I'm Inside, there isn't likely to be any emergency. And in any case, Hofer can handle the communications side."

Clearly what she said made sense. And there was no

reason why she should ever come face to face with Clyne, especially if the man was under his surveillance all the time. "All right," he said, at length. "We'll play it your way. I'll go in at the Northern Sector, and you can handle Ulanov, with Meyer's help. In the meantime, you'd better get Jack Hofer to give you a rundown on using that modified Senso-taper."

CHAPTER THIRTEEN

The Civil Committee were seated at three tables forming a U shape. As an invited guest, rather than an elected member, Gerry Clyne was seated against the far wall at the open end of the U. Listening to the proceedings, he found himself thinking that whoever it was said that a camel was the kind of result one could expect from a committee that set out to design a horse knew what he was talking about. He had been led to understand that the present meeting had been called to consider the appointment of a successor to Brenner as head of military operations for the community, but the discussion seemed to consist in large part of flatulent speeches by those members of the committee whose main qualification for their position was an overfondness for the sound of their own voices.

There had already been several extensive eulogies on the late Colonel Brenner, which, if they had contained even a 50 percent truth content, would have established that undistinguished little man as the greatest military leader since the Duke of Wellington; and now, at last, the discussion was beginning to get around to the question of the appointment of a successor. Torrance had told him that this was the reason for his being invited to the meeting, and his own common sense told him that his work during the past few months had established him as the obvious choice, but he knew in advance that there was sure to be some opposition, and that its focal point would be Magruder, the tall, bony man, with an angry, turkey-cock face who was speaking at the moment.

"... point I want to make about the new leader, whoever he may be, is that he should not lightly embark on any drastic reorganization of policies that have proved so successful in the past." Magruder had a nasal, high-pitched voice with the peculiarly irritating quality of a buzz-saw. "There have been no serious raids during the last two months, and our losses in men and materials have been considerably reduced. This being so, it seems to those of us whose main wish is to get life back to normal that the most fruitful course would be to continue this wise policy of containment within our present perimeter. There seems to us no excuse for any drastic alterations in this policy, and before we vote on the matter in hand, I think we should invite a statement from the candidate telling us what changes he intends to make if he should be elected. Another point I would like to make is that, although Mr. Clyne has been working with Colonel Brenner for some time, his previous experience in the military field is nonexistent. Surely it would be possible to find another, better qualified candidate from amongst the regular army personnel at our disposal?"

"Do I take it that you wish to make an alternative nomination?" asked the chairman of the committee.

"There has hardly been sufficient time to consider alternatives," Magruder said. "But I am sure that there must be several—and that we can only do harm to the common cause if we allow ourselves to be rushed into making a decision which we may regret later. I propose that, rather than run this risk, we adjourn and postpone making any decision in this matter for at least forty-eight hours. It seems to me that ..."

"Mr. Chairman," cut in Torrance, who was seated about the middle of the lefthand table. "While I am fully convinced that Mr. Magruder has the best interests of the community at heart, and that his counsel of caution is well meant, I feel that I must point out that delay in making this appointment could have serious consequences."

"I have the floor!" objected Magruder, his color deepening as he turned on Torrance.

"Yes, Mr. Magruder, and you have had it for a very long

time," Torrance said mildly, as he lumbered to his feet. "The fact that things have been comparatively quiet for some time, far from lulling us into self-congratulation, should put us even more on our guard. It could well be that the guerillas are regrouping and preparing for some new offensive—and what better time to launch such an offensive than when we are without a military commander? This being so, I say that we cannot afford to delay in making this appointment. But, before we go any further, it seems to me sensible that we should be prepared to listen to a statement from a man, who, although he himself would be the first to admit, has not had an extensive military background, has nevertheless distinguished himself in a number of actions during the time he has been here, and has won the trust of myself for one. Whether or not we make any decision after hearing him is a matter for you to decide, but the least we can do after having asked him here this evening is to give him his say."

The chairman nodded, and glanced across at Gerry. "I don't see any objection to your making a statement, if you wish to do so, Mr. Clyne."

Gerry rose to his feet immediately, aware of the angry mutterings of Magruder, who clearly felt that he had been steamrollered by the quiet power of Torrance.

"Thank you, Mr. Chairman, I would like to say a few words," he said. He had not allowed his contempt for this kind of "democratic" time-wasting procedure to prevent his acquiring in the past some measure of skill in handling such bodies, and once on his feet he was sure that he was more than a match for Magruder. "To begin with, can I refer to what Mr. Magruder said about 'getting life back to normal'? I'm not sure that I understand precisely what he means by the use of this word 'normal'—but I would remind all of you here that our enclave within this dome constitutes the major, probably the only, surviving body of human beings on this planet. If he means to imply conditions as they were before the missile war, it must be quite obvious to all of you here that it will never be possible to use the word in that sense again. We cannot—we *must* not—ignore the realities of our situation by imagining that we shall eventually be able to relax into a comfortable existence and forget what has happened. Relaxation of this kind implies stasis—and there can be no such condition in our situation. We must either go forward or back.

"At the moment it is true that we are holding our perimeter against the guerillas with some success. But that is not enough. Whilst it continues to exist, the threat from the guerillas must remain a constant drain on our energies. We can never hope to establish a situation which I would qualify as 'conditional normal,' based on our special position here within the dome, until this problem is settled. With a larger, more efficient military force it would be possible for us to take the offensive without risking the security of our community. Once we can pin the enemy down it will be possible to give him a beating that will convince him his situation is hopeless."

Magruder thumped the table. "You'll never do that! They're fanatics who will go on fighting to the last man."

Clyne shook his head. "No, I refuse to believe that. These are intelligent human beings, and they must know already that even under the present circumstances the most they can hope to do is to continue harrassing us, whilst they are destroyed one by one. In the face of a determined offensive, I believe that they would come to terms."

"Terms, with murderers?" Magruder shouted.

Clyne remained cool. "Let's not lose our sense of proportion in this. They may be murderers, from our point of view, but as far as they are concerned they are doing their duty in attempting to avenge the deaths of millions of their people. Nevertheless, I believe that if we can prove to them that military defeat is inevitable, and that further conflict is pointless, they will accept any reasonable offer we are prepared to make. Under such circumstances we could afford to be generous. Would the Committee prefer that we should pursue a policy of merciless extermination until every guerilla is destroyed? Surely that would prove that we—not they—are the fanatics?"

Gerry sensed from the general murmurings that he had the

backing of most of the committee, although Magruder was silent, eyes downcast. Preparing to press his advantage, he was surprised by an interruption from Torrance, who lumbered to his feet and spoke:

"It seems to me that Clyne's proposal makes sense. Whether you agree with him or not on the definition of 'normal,' it's quite obvious that if we are to build any kind of civilized future for the human race, then we must have unity here inside the dome. For those of you who have reservations about the idea of a new offensive, and the inevitable increase this would bring about in our casualty rate, I would point out that this will only be temporary. Nevertheless, the whole scheme must stand or fall on the validity of Clyne's assumption that the guerillas can be convinced that there is no point in their continuing to fight."

"You don't believe that they can be so convinced?" asked Gerry.

Torrance shrugged massively. "Who can say with certainty what any human being will do in a given situation? The guerillas have been conditioned to this conflict—to most of them its continuation must provide the only true reason for living from day to day. Remember, they know that they have nothing to go back to—no country, no kinfolk. They have, in fact, nothing to lose."

Gerry was puzzled. "Are you arguing in favor of a policy of extermination?" he asked.

"I think you know me sufficiently not to believe that," Torrance said. "I am merely pointing out some of the possible flaws that may exist in a plan which carries as its basic assumption this idea that the guerillas will accept defeat. They may appear to do so, even to the extent of apparently becoming assimilated into our society, but how can we be sure that some of them, at least, will not maintain their alien identity. A saboteur within a community can be even more destructive than a guerilla outside it."

Gerry had to admit to himself that Torrance had a valid point. It was one which he himself had considered, but he had deliberately not mentioned it to the committee, whom he considered quite capable of manufacturing their own prejudices. He found it curious that Torrance should be the one to bring the subject up at this particular time. He had thought of the medic as an ally, but now he was acting as if he had some vested interest in the continuation of the conflict. One thing was certain, if the discussion continued, the introduction of this issue was capable of wrecking his chances of persuading the committee to accept him as military leader. He decided to try a bluff.

Smiling first at Torrance, and then taking in the rest of those present, he said: "Well, gentlemen, it seems to me that I should thank our medical officer for his vote of confidence. From the way he talks about the future assimilation of the guerillas into our community, it is quite evident that he has no doubt about the success of my plans for victory. Of course there will be problems, even when peace comes—but let's get our priorities right. First, and most important, is that we should defeat the enemy. Now—do I have your support in this?"

The semantic trickery of the proposal, with its implication that a vote against Gerry was a vote against the prospect of victory, served its purpose. Even Magruder joined grudgingly in the unanimous show of hands, and there were no further arguments against his appointment as military leader of the northern community.

The satisfaction of having got his own way sustained him through the boredom of the rest of the meeting. He was quite prepared to let them go on talking now. He was already confident of the support of Bub Annersley and other combat veterans. Even after final victory, he planned to maintain a nucleus of such men, because with their backing, true power within the dome would rest in his hands indefinitely.

When the committee adjourned at last, he left alone and walked briskly through the twilight streets of Dome City. City . . . he mused ironically. It was nothing more than a shanty town when compared with the *real* cities outside. Given another five years' building perhaps it would have rivalled them with its spacious modern architecture. The foundations had already been laid for the central buildings when the missile war started, but since that time they had lain untouched, a wasteland of dusty white concrete, marking out in skeletal geometry the outlines of structures that would never now be built.

He wondered about the cities outside. Steel and concrete were certainly more enduring than flesh and bone. Despite the intensity of the missile bombardment, some parts of those cities must have survived. Even if at the moment all of humanity was confined within the dome, there was no reason why this should always remain so. By now the degree of radioactivity outside must have fallen considerably . . . Reemergence, the repopulation of those parts of Earth which were free of harmful radiation, repopulation by people who accepted his authority and control. Gerry Clyne smiled to himself as he approached the front door of his prefab bungalow. He found the prospect of running an entire world strangely exhilarating.

The smile faded as he reminded himself that he was taking too much for granted. Reemergence, yes—but repopulation was something else again. There were no children in Dome City, and as far as he knew no woman in the community had conceived since the missile war. A whole world could not be repopulated by five hundred people, unless those people began to breed again.

In their discussions on the subject even Torrance seemed to be remarkably vague about just when that process was likely to recommence. All the people who had come in from the outside after the beginning of the war had been automatically rendered temporarily sterile during decontamination as a precaution against possible radiation-induced mutation of sperm or ovum. This was reasonable, but the thing that really disturbed Gerry was the fact that not one of the hundred-odd women of child-bearing age who had been inside the dome already had yet conceived. Obviously this was due in most cases to the fact that the women concerned had been fitted with long-term capsules which could be expected to continue secreting contraceptive hormones into the bloodstream until they were eventually completely discharged and the natural cycles of the body took over again. According to Torrance, this process was likely to take anything from a year to eighteen months. This being so, it seemed to Gerry that there should have been at least one such capsule failure by now and a resultant conception. It was surely too much of a coincidence to assume that all such devices had been comparatively freshly implanted when the missile war began.

The truly disturbing factor was that there had been no conception amongst those females who denied ever having been fitted with a hormone capsule. Torrance had been able to offer no real explanation of this, other than to suggest vaguely that such inability to conceive might be at least partially psychological, a result of the traumatic effects of the missile war, perhaps in combination with the subject's unconscious conviction that what remained of humanity must remain imprisoned within the dome for an indefinite period. Similar effects, he reminded Gerry, had been noted in experimental animals forced to spend their lives in a restricted environment. If there was any truth in this theory, it seemed to Gerry that it provided an even more important reason why the war within the dome should be concluded as soon as possible, allowing the community to turn its attention and resources outwards.

It was dim in the small hallway of his bungalow, but he did not switch on the light, because he intended to go straight through to the back of the building. Still preoccupied with his somber thoughts, he had pushed the front door shut behind him and was about to walk away when he sensed, rather than saw, a shadowy figure in the corner.

Whirling, reaching for his gun, he was already too late. The revolver butt was only an inch out of its holster when he heard the sharp pop of a hypo-gun.

Consciousness shattered soundlessly and he fell into black nothingness. . . .

CHAPTER FOURTEEN

Avram Meyer was lying on his side in a depression of broken earth newly torn from the ground by the explosion of the mine. Both of his hands were clasped to his belly, feeling the hot, pulsing wetness of the spilled intestines that tried to force their way between his protecting fingers. There was no pain yet. He guessed that he was still protected by the effects of the initial shock. But it seemed that he was to be denied the refuge of unconsciousness, and there would be pain to come.

Somewhere nearby he could hear the rattle of automatic weapons, and the voice of Warrant Officer Gorst roaring orders. The others of the party had got through the minefield and were pressing home the attack. Perhaps, on the way back, they would have time to attend to his needs, or perhaps, hopefully, his present situation had been registered and noted by a monitor back in the Control Dome, and a pickup squad was already on its way through the underground to the nearest entry point.

Perhaps . . . but all he could do was wait, wait here until the pain began. He wanted to look down, to see the nature of the mess that was seeping between his fingers, but he resisted the temptation, because he knew that if he did, he would begin to scream, and that once he had begun, he would not be able to stop . . .

"Avram . . . Avram!" A familiar voice, close to his ear. A hand, gentle on his shoulder. "Avram!"

He awoke, to find his hands clasped to a belly slimed with sweat—to the knowledge that he was lying on the hard bed in his own quarters. The last patrol into the minefield had taken place over a week before, and he had returned unscathed. He shifted, whimpering his relief, and opened his eyes to the dimness.

"Avram," the voice spoke again, and he turned his eyes,

looking into the face of a woman who smiled down at him compassionately.

"Laura! You . . . here . . . ?" He started up on the bed.

"Quietly!" she whispered, one hand to her lips. Her slim body was encased in a black leotard that merged with the dimness of the room, her fair hair hidden by a black cap and her face smeared with dark makeup. There was a belt and holster at her waist, and a webbing harness held a large pack on her back.

He swung his thin legs over the edge of the narrow bed and sat facing her, the horror of the nightmare still jittering his limbs. At the same time, a half-acknowledged, fearful hope was growing in him that her presence was a signal that it was all over—the reality and the nightmare—that she had come to tell him that he could at last leave here and go back to the quiet, shining corridors of the Control Dome, away from this bloody, dirty hell.

"We're . . . we're going back?" His voice was pleading.

"Soon, but not yet." She eased the pack from her shoulders onto the floor. "There are some things we must do first . . . you and I together. I told you that you would be needed when the time came—and the time is *now*."

Disappointment and shame flooded through him. Disappointment that this was not to be the quick escape he had hoped for—and shame at his own lack of courage as compared with this strong, attractive lioness of a woman. "I don't understand . . ."

"I couldn't tell you the full plan earlier, but now I will explain. Davidson is already in the Northern Sector. He has . . ."

He listened as she told him the whole story, hope growing in him as he understood that with the success of such a plan the violence Inside would be ended. "But the Director—surely he will realize that there is something unusual happening when he gets his reports from the Monitor Section?" he said, when she paused at last.

"There will be no reports from Monitor Section," she said. "There will be a blackout on all video circuits between Inside and Control. With Hofer and his men on our side there can be no rectifying of that fault for at least twenty-four hours, but we must move quickly. My task is to prepare Ulanov for a meeting with Clyne from the Northern Sector, and I shall need your help.''

''You will trigger his true memory in the same way Davidson is doing with Clyne?''

She shook her head. ''Ulanov has no true memory. It was erased when he was programmed. His only reality is the situation here Inside. The original intention was that he should be replaced by another man especially programmed by Davidson, but there is no time for that now. He must be prepared by another method to accept the idea of a truce.''

''Ulanov?'' Meyer stared at her in astonishment. ''But you can't understand! Ulanov is completely dedicated to the task of destroying the northern community. No arguments you may bring could possibly convince him.''

''We shall not rely on *arguments*,'' she said firmly. She pointed to the pack which lay on the floor. ''That is a modified Senso-taper with a specially prepared programme tape which must be fed into his mind.''

''He would never submit to such treatment.''

''I have drugs. He must be made to accept.''

''And if we fail?''

''Then Ulanov will have to be removed and you will take command in this section.''

''Impossible! Gorst and the others . . . you can have no idea . . .''

''We must create our own possibilities, Avram.''

He shook his head, still doubtful. ''I still think it's hopeless.''

''If necessary, I shall perform the task alone,'' she said. ''Understand, I cannot order you to participate in this plan if you do not wish it, but I am committed. If you wish, you have every right to walk out of here and go back to Control through the nearest underground entry point. No blame will attach to you.''

''And if you fail?''

''Complete Erasure and Reconditioning. Moule would not hesitate, in the face of such rebellion against his domination.''

He saw that she was in deadly earnest, and her implacable bravery shamed him. He had complained for so long about the suffering and misery of the people Inside. How could he fail to play his part now, when there was a chance of ending that misery forever? If he did so, how could he ever hope to look at his own face again in a mirror without feeling disgust?

"All right, Laura," he said. "What do you want me to do?"

CHAPTER FIFTEEN

The smoke from the fire ceased to climb. It remained static for a moment, then made a complete change of direction and began to flow back downwards towards the flames. It snuffed them out, to reveal the blackness of charred wood beneath, then the blackness faded and the sticks were once again clean, uncharred wood, forming the carefully arranged nest of the potential fire. Instantly the nest disintegrated, as the sticks, moving in an intricate complex of spatial patterns, fitted raw edge against raw edge and knitted together until they once again formed the perfect natural relationship that was the tree branch.

Gerry Clyne opened his eyes. He was seated in an armchair in the lounge of his own bungalow. A man with a lean, ascetic face sat opposite him in the other chair. Somehow Gerry knew that this man's name was Davidson —Michael Davidson— and that he was a Programmer.

A Programmer? What is a Programmer?

The question was like a shot fired in a quiet forest. Chaos . . . Confusion . . . Like screaming, startled animals, thought chains scurried in all directions through his mind. Body shaking in response to an uncontrollable panic reaction, he half-rose from the chair, fighting the overwhelming terror of a disorientation that threatened his sanity.

A face loomed over him. Still struggling against the splintering horror, he became aware of physical contact as hands pushed him firmly back into the chair.

"Take it easy, Clyne. Don't try too hard. Just let it find its own level, and don't resist. Trust me, and all your questions will be answered eventually."

Trust me . . . The forest of mind was quietening gradually, as he looked to the vaguely benevolent image of the pale, bony face for meaning, stability.

"The human mind can only stand so much reality"—the quotation drifted into his consciousness unbidden. And following closely, a question: *"What of a mind faced by two realities?"*

Memory was there at the touch of a thought, memory of the shelter, of the fire, and the charred thing that had once been Kay; of those terrible days of the missile war in which a whole world of human beings had died.

"Where . . . ?" he began, and stopped, because he already knew the answer to his question as *other* memories coalesced and made a meaningful pattern. He remembered his arrest by the Socio/Psyche Department officers, the hearing before the examining board, and the verdict. Then the sentence, pronounced by the solemn-faced chairman of the examining board, a sentence which had meant his transportation here to . . .

"Mars!" he said, tasting the bitter hopelessness of the single syllable.

Davidson nodded. "Yes, Mars. Inside the controlled environment, programmed like all the other subjects in here to accept this as your reality. But in your case there is a difference, because I left your basic memories intact, so that they could be triggered back into full awareness."

"Then the missile war—the destruction of the major part of the human race . . ."

"It stumbled to the edge of that particular abyss a number of times, but something, call it God, or good fortune, has always pulled it or them back from the brink. Outside this dome, apart from Control, there is nothing but the airless wastes of Mars. And back on Earth, the overcrowded planet you remember—stifled by overpopulation, inward-looking and without purpose."

"I had purpose," Gerry said.

"Lust for money, power, women?" Davidson's thin

92

© Lorillard 1974

King Size
or Deluxe 100's.

KENT

WITH
THE FAMOUS MICRONITE FILTER

DELUXE LENGTH

If you have
a taste for quality,
you'll like the taste
of Kent.

Kings: 16 mg. "tar," 1.0 mg. nicotine;
100's: 18 mg. "tar," 1.2 mg. nicotine
av. per cigarette, FTC Report Mar. '74

© Lorillard 1974

Try the crisp, clean taste
of Kent Menthol 100's.
The only Menthol with the famous Micronite filter.

mouth twisted contemptuously. "Society can no longer afford people with such purposes."

"I've heard all those arguments before, at the hearing," Gerry said. "All right, so I'm a criminal, a psychotic, like all the others here; but at the same time I'm different, because I know where I really am. Why me? What good does it do to let the experimental animal know what he is, to let him understand that his life can be snuffed out by forces greater than himself at any time?"

"But surely that is the natural condition of Man?" Davidson said. "We are, always have been, vulnerable, whatever puny advances we may make into the darkness."

Gerry was more alert now, his mind concentrating on more practical, immediate questions than the metaphysical ones raised by Davidson. "The war that is going on in here—this bloody battling with the guerillas. You're not trying to tell me that's somebody's idea of therapy."

"Many of us dislike the way the Director has been running things Inside, and we disagree with his policies . . ."

"You *dislike*?" Gerry felt the muscles of his face twisting in an involuntary expression of his disgust and rage. "But you're a Programmer. How many human minds have you filled with false reality, and sent them in here to die? What is it—some kind of a game? If so, it beats anything the ancient Romans ever dreamed up."

"Most don't die; or if they do, they're brought out to the Control Dome and revived, given surgery and reprogrammed."

"You mean they aren't even allowed the dignity of dying once and finally?"

"I didn't invent the system," said Davidson. "You ask why you're different—*that's* the reason. It's going to be changed, and you're the one who will change it, with our help."

It was still an odd sensation to be possessed of a mind that insisted on the equal validity of two differing memory patterns, but now at least he knew why the condition existed, and with this knowledge he found himself gaining in confidence. With the help of this new assurance, he found himself looking more acutely at Davidson, and evaluating what he

93

saw. There was intelligence in the lean face, and sincerity
—but there was something else, flickering just beneath the
surface of those overintense eyes, betraying itself in the
barely repressed agitation which lent a tremor to the man's
long-fingered, bony hands and kindled a tic at the corner of
the thin-lipped mouth. Whatever Davidson's skills and
knowledge, it was clear to Gerry that he was dealing with a
man obsessed to the point of fanaticism.

"Tell me more," he said quietly. "Tell me just how it is,
and how it's going to be changed."

"The controlled environment project is under the directorship of a man called Moule, who is answerable only to the
central Socio/Psyche Council back on Earth," said Davidson. "He has been in charge here since the project's incep-
tion, some five years ago."

"Five years . . . Now just a minute," interrupted Gerry.
He told Davidson about the unresolved inconsistency which
had come up during his first meeting with Brenner, when
Brenner had mentioned that the time elapsed since the missile
war was six months, when he himself had been of the opinion
that it was little more than four weeks.

Davidson nodded. "That is perfectly normal. It is caused
by a process instigated during Programming, which causes a
contraction and blurring of memory beyond a period of a few
months."

"Like blasted chickens!" explained Gerry.

"Chickens?" Davidson's eyebrows rose.

"Don't they teach you basic Psyche any more? A
chicken—domestic fowl—found by experimentation to have
a twenty-minute memory. Rabbits, too. A quick memory
decay rate is a matter of survival in their case. They are
subject to so many dangers from predators in the natural state
that the damned things would just lie down and die in a
psychotic trance if they were capable of remembering."

"Yes, I see. The reference eluded me at first," Davidson
said. "I was telling you about Moule. As Director, he had a
completely free hand to set up Inside—that's what we call the
controlled environment, by the way—according to whatever
dramatic premises he considered would be most fruitful in his

94

researches. This being so, he began by laying down a basic situation that would be common to all subjects within the environment.''

"The missile war.''

"Precisely. It was his initial theory that the provision of such a common hinterland of experience would serve as a unifying influence on the people Inside, and also have the added advantage of making them accept the necessity of remaining within the environment.''

"That seems reasonable enough," Gerry said.

"Yes, and it might have worked, if he had been dealing with normal human beings rather than criminal psychotics," said Davidson. "As it was, violence broke out in the community within the first three months, and it soon became quite clear that even with the constant intervention of Role-Players, such a society could not possibly attain any kind of stability, and must eventually destroy itself. In order to avoid this, Moule conceived the idea of introducing a "guerilla force," which was supposed to have landed near to Dome City and invaded it through the southern entrance during the first days of the missile war. The introduction of this new element, plus a certain reprogramming of key subjects served to provide the unifying element that was needed, producing two groups, the aggression of each of which was channelled in the direction of the other, rather that self-destructively inward. The sides were carefully balance—the north, with its numerical superiority, was handicapped by the fact that its military operations were directed by a negative nonentity, Brenner. The guerillas, on the other hand, had a first-class leader, Ulanov, but were short on the men and materials they needed to gain a decisive victory. Such a position of stalemate required a minimum of intervention on the part of Role-Players for its maintenance, and would probably have remained in existence indefinitely if we had not decided it must be changed.''

"We?" queried Clyne.

"A group of people working in the Control Dome who have become progressively more sickened by the continued butchery resulting from the present situation Inside, and who

95

are determined to create a different one. No one back on Earth was prepared to listen to us, so we had no alternative but to take matters into our own hands."

The whole thing sounded like a standard, idealistic revolutionary argument to Gerry, and even on the little information he had, he found himself doubting its practicality. "And this 'different' dramatic situation—what makes you think that you will be able to maintain it, where Moule's original efforts failed?"

"For one thing, we're not satisfied that Moule really did fail," Davidson said. "Or at least, that if he did, we believe that failure may have been intentional, engineered deliberately so that he could justify the situation he had already planned to establish to the Socio/Psyche Council. Moule is a strange man—even those who have worked with him in close association find themselves unable to make any really intimate contact. He is remote, removed from any social intercourse with the rest of us."

"The loneliness of command," suggested Gerry. "After all, in a position like his, a certain amount of remoteness must be necessary if one is to maintain discipline."

"But this is supposed to be a Socio/Psyche experimental project, not a military campaign," Davidson said. "Discipline, in the sense you're talking about, doesn't enter into the situation."

It was Gerry's private opinion that discipline of one kind or another entered into *any* situation involving human beings, but he let the argument lie. The main thing at the moment was to get as much information as possible from Davidson. "All right," he said. "Given the fact you and your group don't accept the reasons Moule professes for setting up this conflict between the Dome City community and the guerillas, you must have at least theorized about the nature of his true motives."

"We believe that the only possible answer is that he is dangerously unbalanced; that he has developed a paranoid system of delusions which convinces him of a godlike infallibility—this, coupled with a sadistic drive of similar proportions. Look at it this way—he holds the power of life and death, of resurrection even, over nearly a thousand human beings. What more satisfying toy could a paranoid possess?''

Clyne frowned. ''It seems to me that if this were true, there should be some way of demonstrating its truth to the authorities back on Earth.''

''That is what we had hoped, in the first instance,'' Davidson said, ''but it has proved totally impossible. I myself have sent tapes back to Earth to people in whom I have the utmost trust, but with completely negative results. I can only assume that they were tampered with before arrival. Even though Mars may be remote to anyone living on Earth, I find it impossible to believe that my correspondents would have ignored my appeals in this way.''

''All right, assuming that your tapes have been interfered with, what about those people from Control who have gone back to Earth?''

''There are not many. Most of us are on long-term contracts, but some have gone back for one reason or another from time to time.''

''And?''

Davidson shrugged his bony shoulders. ''In each case, although they have promised to keep in touch, and do what they can, nothing more has been heard from them. Either they have been deliberately silenced, or when they arrived back on Earth our problems here on Mars no longer seemed important to them. Faced by such a situation, our only possible course was to take direct action ourselves.''

''I see,'' Clyne said. ''But surely, from what you have told me of the Control set-up, I understood that everything that goes on here Inside is monitored.''

''That is true,'' Davidson said. ''There are hundreds of static concealed sound and vision cameras, as well as a large number of self-propelled micros, all of which are controlled by the Monitor Section.''

''Then surely it follows that we are being watched at this moment, and that Moule must already know about your plan?''

''Normally this would be so,'' Davidson said. ''But one of the members of our group, the head of Electronics Section, has arranged an apparently accidental communications blackout. Before the necessary 'repairs' are effected, we shall have changed the situation Inside irrevocably."

"How will you do this?"

"The first essential is to bring an end to the conflict between the Dome City community and the guerillas," Davidson said. "This was one of the main reasons for the unusual nature of your own programming. You had the natural leadership potential we required; and I calculated that with some assistance you would be capable of taking over military control of the community."

Assistance . . . Recognition dawned on Gerry. "Is Torrance one of your Role-Players?"

"Yes. It was his task to help pave the way for your assumption of power."

"Then why isn't he here now?" Gerry asked.

"You misunderstand," Davidson said. "Torrance is a Role-Player, and he has helped in your takeover, but he is not a member of our group. As far as he is concerned, he has been merely acting on instructions which he believes to have come from the Director."

Gerry considered the bewildering ramifications of intrigue so far revealed to him by Davidson. Apparently his assumption of military leadership in the northern community was a prerequisite of the entire scheme, whatever that might be, but there were still a number of aspects that he did not understand. Clearly Davidson was a monomaniac, who assumed that other people would automatically accept his infallibility and not question any orders he cared to give, but it was not in Gerry's nature to trust so blindly in the judgment of others—especially in that of a person whose stability he instinctively doubted. Torrance, even before he acquired this new dimension of being recognized as a Role-Player, was easily identified as a person of some importance, with qualities that commanded respect and attention. Davidson, on the other hand . . .

"Obviously I can know nothing about the procedure involved in such matters," Gerry said, "but how will you account for your presence here when you meet Torrance?"

"That is unimportant, for the moment," Davidson said impatiently. "He will be dealt with. Now, it is essential that you should understand what is required of you. From the monitor reports I have seen on your activities I know that you have already decided that no progress can be made within the dome until the conflict with the guerillas has been concluded.''

"That is true.''

"Your plan entailed an all-out offensive and complete victory,'' Davidson said. "Such action will now, of course, be quite unnecessary. I am expecting to hear shortly from a colleague, who is contacting the guerilla leader.''

"Then I'm not unique, after all? Ulanov too has been given this double-Programming?''

Davidson frowned. "No, unfortunately that was not possible. It was our intention that he should be replaced later by another subject who had been suitably conditioned, but the execution of our plan has been put forward.''

The implications of this carefully vague explanation did not escape Gerry. Despite his show of confidence, Davidson was evidently not in complete control of the situation. He was under some kind of pressure.

"Ulanov's second-in-command is one of our Role-Players,'' Davidson said. "Another member of our group has gone into guerilla territory to assist him. These two have the necessary apparatus to perform a temporary reprogramming of Ulanov. Once this has been done, it is merely a matter of arranging a meeting between him and yourself, as the two military leaders. When that has been achieved, it should be a simple matter to organize the unification of the population of Inside.''

"That seems logical—particularly when the people of both north and south sectors realize that the conflict in the past has been completely without point,'' Gerry said. "In fact, I would have thought that your manner of going about this entire operation is unnecessarily devious. If your group has access to all the communications channels at the disposal of Control, then surely the obvious thing to do would have been to arrange a mass dissemination of the true facts of their existence to all the people within the Dome? Once everyone knew these facts, there would clearly be no possibility of the conflict continuing.''

Davidson's eyes widened. "Good God, man! Do you realize what you're suggesting? You can't really imagine that we would place such knowledge in the hands of several hundred dangerous psychotics. Our intention is to bring about a stabilized, more humane situation within the environment, but that situation must remain subject to our control."

Gerry refrained from making the obvious comment that he himself was one of those dangerous psychotics to whom Davidson referred. He still had a great deal to learn about Davidson, his group, and the precise nature of the Control structure, but his alert mind was already exploring certain possibilities, the nature of which he had no intention of revealing at this stage.

"I see," he said calmly. "Then it is your intention that this knowledge will be confined to myself and Ulanov?"

"Naturally."

"In that case, what makes you so sure that the population of the Dome will be prepared to accept an apparently arbitrary truce arranged between myself and Ulanov?"

Davidson smiled thinly. "My dear fellow, surely that is quite obvious? Both of you have been established as strong and popular leaders in your respective communities. The people will do as you say. In fact they will be pleased to do so, because most of them must be heartily sick of the constant attrition of the war situation."

Gerry nodded. "That seems a reasonable assumption. But how and where am I to meet Ulanov? He can hardly walk through the carefully guarded perimeter of our defenses without being shot by our sentries, nor can I go into guerilla-held territory without running the same danger."

"Neither of those risks will be necessary," Davidson said. "How do you imagine that I myself got here without being stopped by your own guards?" He glanced at his wrist watch. "I think it is time we were leaving."

"Now wait a minute," Gerry said. "How do I know that this isn't some kind of trap?"

Davidson gave a dry chuckle. "Trap? To what purpose? If I'd wanted to kill you I could have done that easily enough earlier on."

"All right, I'll give you that much," Gerry said. "But I'd still like to know where we're supposed to be going."

"For a meeting with Ulanov, naturally." Davidson pointed to the gun which was still in its holster at Clyne's hip. "By the way, you'd better leave that here. We don't want any misunderstandings at this stage. This will be a peaceful meeting."

"I hope you know what you're doing," Gerry said, removing the weapon belt with some reluctance, and placing it out of sight in a cupboard.

"I think so," said Davidson. "Now, shall we go?"

Outside, darkness had fallen over the dome, and the streets of prefabricated buildings were lit by bluish fluorotubes strung overhead at irregular intervals. They saw the odd lone stroller, but at this time of the evening most of the inhabitants of this section were clustered in the main entertainment centers around the central-square. Avoiding that area, they travelled in a northeasterly direction, arriving some ten minutes later at the metal fencing that guarded the nuclear power plant which provided electricity for the community.

Gerry watched without comment as Davidson produced a key which opened a small side gate and let them into the compound. The power plant was computer-controlled, and self-repairing, which meant that it was seldom visited, except for the occasional inspection by the chief power engineer. Gerry himself had never before been inside the place, but it was obviously familiar to Davidson. He led the way through the main control room of the building and into a storeroom beyond. Here, stacked on metal shelving which reached to the ceiling some twelve feet above, were varied components which he guessed had been intended for use in the installations to be made within the buildings of the main city. Beyond the shelving, at the far end of the room, was another door. This opened onto a cubicle-sized office, sparsely furnished with a desk, a chair, and a voice-writer.

Glancing back to make sure that Gerry was close behind him, Davidson produced a penlike object from his pocket and placed it against an extension socket on the side of the desk. There was a brief humming, then the floor of the room dropped away rapidly beneath their feet.

101

A few seconds later they stepped off the elevator/office into a well-lit semispherical chamber with four circular tunnels about two meters in diameter leading from it. In the center of the room stood a four-wheeled vehicle with accommodation for two passengers.

Davidson got into the driving seat, and Gerry took his place beside him. The motor hummed into life at the press of a button, and Davidson steered it towards one of the tunnels. Gerry sat silently as they moved with gathering speed through what he guessed to be part of the underground network which honeycombed the foundations of Inside, and—the thought kindled an anticipatory thrill in his mind—must undoubtedly connect Inside with the Control Dome. . . .

CHAPTER SIXTEEN

The ability to sleep automatically, at odd hours and under any circumstances, was one which Colonel Nikilai Ulanov had trained in himself during his many years of active service. But tonight, for no positively identifiable reason, that ability failed him and he found himself in a state of hyper-alertness that made relaxation impossible. He had experienced this kind of feeling before. It was almost like a kind of Psionic awareness, a clairvoyance that told him something was about to happen, but did not define the nature of that something. He could feel the tension of the impending event in the very air he breathed, sense it all around him as he paced the floor of his headquarters, smoking one thin black cigar after another.

Once, he walked out onto the verandah, where he nodded to the sentry and went into the radio room. At a gesture from his commanding officer the corporal on duty remained in his seat. They listened together for several minutes to the quiet hiss of the carrier wave in the overhead loudspeaker, then Ulanov nodded his dismissal and walked back to his own room. Seated at his desk, he attempted to occupy himself with the drafting of orders for the following day. But his mind would not concentrate on the routine task, attuned as it was by the unbidden presence of the soldier's sixth sense which had saved his life only a few weeks previously, prompting him to take one path, rather than another, only to discover afterwards that the original one had been mined.

Many had died since the beginning of this campaign, and many more would do so; but all these deaths were insignificant compared with the massive, impersonal slaughter of the missile war. Impersonal . . . no, it could never be that from his point of view. As a soldier he was used to seeing the death of comrades, other soldiers. The goal of final victory could serve as some justification for such deaths, but he found himself haunted by the knowledge that whatever victory he might win here, within the closed world of the dome, there could never be any comfort against the memory that Nadia and little Pyotr had died in the flaming, radioactive hell of Kiev.

The sound of the sentry's feet slamming to attention broke in on his morose thoughts. He looked up as the door opened to admit Captain Meyer, who was followed by a tall woman, whose strikingly handsome features were daubed with black greasepaint. The woman was wearing a figure-hugging black suit, and she carried a canvas pack, slung by a webbing strap from her right shoulder.

"Captain?" Ulanov's body tensed as he faced the pair, his eyes resting warily on the strange woman. "Who is this?"

Meyer, obviously nervous, made no reply, but the woman stepped forward boldly. "My name is Frayne, Laura Frayne," she said in a calm, precise voice. "I have just arrived from outside the dome."

"That is impossible," Ulanov said, his tension increasing. "Nothing, no one could exist out there after all this time. Who is this woman?" he demanded from Meyer. It seemed likely to him that she was a spy from the Northern Sector, but if that was the case how could Meyer have been so stupid as to bring her here?

"Colonel Ulanov, it would be better if you were to listen to what I have to tell you." The voice of the woman was firm, but her amber eyes held a strange gentleness.

Even so, Ulanov was now convinced that this must be the

situation of which his danger-sense had been giving him vague warnings. This woman, brought here by Meyer . . . He leapt out of his chair, the cry that would raise the alarm already bubbling in his throat.

A gleaming, metallic object appeared in the hand of the woman, and there was a brief pop, like the sound of a cork being removed from a bottle. The cry died on Ulanov's lips as he tumbled forward into oblivion.

Laura replaced the hypo gun in its holster as Ulanov crumpled to the floor, and moved swiftly to the door to the right of the commander's desk. In the small room beyond, she discarded the heavy pack, then returned immediately. She bent down, grasping Ulanov's legs.

"Come on!" she whispered urgently to Meyer, who was still standing, a dazed expression on his face. "We have to get him into his sleeping quarters, where I can work on him."

Meyer hesitated. "The sentry," he said.

"He heard nothing, or he would have been in here by now. Move, Avram, move!"

Meyer obeyed, grasping the prostrate form beneath the shoulders. Ulanov was a powerfully built man, and it was no easy task to drag the limp form through to the sleeping quarters and place it on the bed. Laura bent over her pack, unzipping its fastenings, as she said to Meyer: "You can go back into the office and leave this to me. Your main job is to make sure that I'm not disturbed during the Reprogramming.

"Gorst will probably call in later, when the guard changes," Meyer said uneasily. "He usually makes a personal report to Ulanov at that time."

"Then you must tell him that the Colonel is sleeping, and has left you in charge for the time being."

"But if the sentry has told him about you . . ."

"Oh, for God's sake, Avram!" She wheeled on him impatiently. "Improvise something, can't you? Tell him Ulanov asked you to bring him a woman—surely that's simple enough?"

"Not Ulanov. You don't understand. He would never . . ."

"All right, then tell him some other story. But now get out

and leave me to work!'' Laura said, lifting the modified Senso-taper out of the pack.

Meyer looked at the unconscious form of Ulanov, the strong features relaxed, slightly softened by the dulling effect of the anaesthetic, and felt guilt at his own treachery. This man had trusted him . . .

''Avram!''

Laura's voice galvanized him into action. Leaving the inner room, he walked carefully across to the outer door and listened. The sentry was still at his post. Wiping his perspiration-dampened hands on the front of his shirt, Meyer moved back and sat down behind Ulanov's desk to wait.

He tried to tell himself that it was absurd he should feel this sense of guilt. After Reprogramming Ulanov would understand that the whole thing had been done for his own good, and that of the other people Inside. But even then, surely this had been a betrayal? There should have been some other way . . .

He found himself comparing his own nervous hesitation with the direct courage of Laura Frayne. Perhaps he would have found the whole thing easier if he had been conditioned to acceptance of the idea earlier, but on top of his guilt, he found himself nervously aware of the possible pitfalls of the plan. Davidson was bringing Clyne through the underground to meet Ulanov, and Laura seemed quite confident that with this meeting the conflict Inside would come to an automatic halt. Meyer found it impossible to share her confidence. Even though Ulanov himself might be Reprogrammed, it was difficult to imagine that anything could override the emotional power of the bitterness that the years of conflict had built up amongst the rank and file fighters on both sides. Warrant Officer Gorst, for instance, was hardly likely to accept, even from Ulanov, orders to abandon the fight that had given his life its main purpose for so long. And Gorst must have his counterparts in the northern community. It might have been possible to bring about some kind of stable peace if all the people Inside were made aware of the true reality of the situation; but such a thing could only be achieved by the Reprogramming of each and every person

Inside, a task which was completely out of the question within the time limits of this operation. As it was, the whole scheme would stand or fall on the power of Ulanov and Clyne over the people of their respective sectors. If their authority was challenged, then the entire structure might well crumble.

He looked at his watch. Only ten minutes now to the change of guards. He glanced back towards the closed door of the inner room, wondering how Laura's work was progressing, but not daring to go in and disturb her in order to find out.

Rising from behind the desk, he began to pace the floor. If only there were something positive he could do, rather than just waiting . . .

Heavy footsteps outside, and the slamming of the sentry's feet as a familiar barking voice shouted an order. A moment later the outer door opened and Gorst walked in, erect body whipping to attention in a salute.

"The Comrade Colonel?" The eyes of the black-bearded giant betrayed surprise.

"He is resting," Meyer said. "You can give me your report."

"With respect, the Comrade Colonel's specific instructions . . . If he is asleep, I am expected to awaken him."

"Why? Is there any emergency?"

"No, Comrade Captain, nevertheless. . ."

"The Colonel has been slightly unwell, but he is resting now. There is no point in disturbing him in order to deliver a routine report."

The big warrant officer hesitated, a frown of bafflement on his bearded face.

"I shall tell him you were here, don't worry about that, Gorst," Meyer said.

The warrant officer's enormous, muscular body still remained erect to attention. Meyer, some ten centimeters shorter, faced him, attempting to display a confidence that he did not feel. "You may go now, Gorst!" he said sharply.

The bluff might have worked if at that precise moment there had not been a slight sound of movement from behind the door of the commander's sleeping quarters. Both men heard the sound, but it was Gorst who moved into action.

Thrusting past Meyer, he dived for the door and flung it open. Ulanov lay on the narrow bed, the top of his head covered by the shining white plastic of the induction cap, multiple-cored, color-coded cable sprouting from its crown and leading down to the portable Senso-taper. The dark-suited form of Laura Frayne was bent over the instrument, making fine adjustments as its reels moved, feeding tape slowly past the playing heads.

"Avram!" Laura looked up, startled by the intrusion.

Her exclamation was drowned by a bull-like roar of fury as Gorst's two hundred-and-twenty-pound body launched forward into the confined space of the room.

Meyer was close behind, aiming a chop to the back of the warrant officer's treelike neck, but the other shrugged off the blow as he ripped the induction cap from the head of his unconscious commander. Driven by panic, he put all his force behind a second blow to Gorst's kidneys, but it had no effect. Flailing the induction cap by its connecting cable, the warrant officer smashed it down on the Senso-taper. Plastic crumpled, and the movement of the reels ceased.

He turned to face Meyer, the light of battle in his eyes. Aware that he was no match for this mountain of a man in unarmed combat, Meyer was tugging at his gun when a smashing blow connected with the side of his head. Consciousness blurred . . .

He struggled back to full awareness of his surroundings to see the figure of Gorst huddled over the smashed remains of the Senso-taper. Ulanov was still unconscious on the bed, but there was no sign of Laura Frayne, and the door of the room was closed.

Getting to his feet, he drew the automatic from his holster and approached the door cautiously. From beyond he heard the sharp, unmistakable pop of a hypo gun.

He eased the door open cautiously, his gun ready. Laura was standing over the prone body of the sentry, the hypo in her right hand. She turned towards him.

"You're all right, Avram? Good! Give me a hand with this one, will you?"

They dragged the unconscious man into the back room, which was now beginning to have the look of an over-crowded morgue.

Laura made a brief examination of the mangled Senso-taper. When she looked up her face was grim. "We'll get no more help from that thing," she said.

"I tried to stop Gorst," Meyer said, humiliatingly aware of the apologetic weakness of his voice.

"Yes, sure you did." Laura was adjusting the control dial on her hypo gun. She turned back towards Ulanov, who still lay unmoving.

"What are you going to do?" Meyer asked.

"What else is there? I shall have to revive Ulanov and hope that he had a chance to assimilate sufficient of that tape. If so, it may be possible to talk sense with him. If not . . ." She shrugged. Levelling the hypo gun at Ulanov, she fired a stimulant shot directly into his heart.

Ten, fifteen seconds went by before the body on the bed stirred. A moaning sound issued from the mouth, then quite suddenly it jerked upright into a sitting position. Ulanov's eyes opened, to reveal a crazy emptiness, and a drool of saliva spilled from the corner of his slack mouth as he mumbled incoherently.

Meyer stared horrified at the moronic creature on the bed. "What's happened, for God's sake?"

"I was afraid of this," Laura said. "The sudden break, when Gorst wrenched the induction cap from his head, was too much for him to take. His mind was in a hyper-receptive state, with not sufficient of the tape assimilated to provide him with a firm basis for rationality. He's in a state of deep traumatic shock."

"But there must be something you can do," Meyer said.

"With that thing?" Laura gestured in the direction of the ruined Senso-taper. "Not a hope. He'll remain that way until he gets proper treatment. The only thing I can do is put him out again, until he can be taken back to Control for complete Erasure and Reconditioning."

Meyer watched as the hypo gun popped again and the moaning figure lapsed back into unconsciousness. "But surely he was essential to your plan?"

Laura nodded firmly. "He *was*."

Meyer's tongue moved over dry lips. "What can we do now?" he asked.

"I shall have to go to the underground entry point and discuss the situation with Davidson."

"But I thought that I was supposed to take Ulanov there," said Meyer.

"You were—but that's hardly possible now, is it? We'll have to change tactics. I'll call Control from the underground, and arrange for a pickup squad to get these three out. In the meantime you'll have to take over here."

"Me?" Meyer said shakily.

"Of course *you*," Laura affirmed. "Who else is there?"

"But tomorrow—when the men start asking questions. . ."

Laura's mouth tightened. "For God's sake get a grip on yourself, Avram. You'll be in command here for the time being, that's all. As far as the men are concerned, you have to tell them that Ulanov and Gorst have disappeared. Nobody's going to suspect you, as Ulanov's second in command. You don't have have to explain anything."

"But the man in the radio room. . ."

"If he'd heard anything he would have raised the alarm already," Laura said. "All you've got to do for the time being is to keep things under control in this sector. Surely you can manage that?"

Meyer nodded his head uncertainly. "For how long?"

"I can't tell you that, can I? First I have to talk to Davidson."

Meyer avoided her eyes. "All right, I'll do my best," he said, without conviction. It seemed to him that nothing but disaster could come from this night's work.

CHAPTER SEVENTEEN

Davidson glanced anxiously at his watch for the tenth time since they had arrived at the meeting point.

"I hear this Ulanov is a pretty tough handful," Gerry said casually. "Maybe your people are having trouble with him?"

"Nonsense! There are two of them, and they have the necessary equipment," Davidson said.

Gerry guessed that he had touched on a raw spot of uncertainty, but he felt no qualm about pursuing a line that allowed him to explore the reactions of the other. He had already formed the opinion that, although Davidson might have persuaded others, even himself, that he had embarked on this adventure in order to frcc the people Inside from the constant uncertainty and suffering of the guerilla war, what he was really seeking was the opportunity of placing himself in a position of power over the entire Mars project. Men like Davidson craved power, like spoiled children trying to dominate their contemporaries—and if that power was denied them, they fell into an infantile pattern of destructive hysteria. The real problem in dealing with such an unstable personality was to make sure that any such destructive outbursts should be directed inward, rather than against other people. Gerry found himself wondering how the others who were supposedly working with Davidson could have failed to recognize the potential dangers in following such a leader.

"I don't understand why only you and this Frayne girl came Inside," Gerry said. "Surely a larger group would have been able to handle the situation more easily and efficiently?"

"No—that's the point," Davidson said irritably. "It is essential that we do as little as possible to upset the subjective reality of the people Inside."

"To keep them in the situation of puppets, you mean?"

"They have to remain here, whatever the outcome, and

they are more likely to accept their lives if the basic premises concerning the reason for their being Inside remain unaltered. That makes sense, surely?''

''If you accept the assumption that they should remain here in captivity, like animals in a zoo,'' replied Gerry. ''You must appreciate that, as one of them, I find such a concept humiliating.''

Davidson glanced at him sharply. ''That may be so, but you have little alternative. There can be no question of your people being allowed to go back to Earth. In any case, I can't see that you, in particular, should have any cause for complaint.''

''You mean that I should be content to accept the role of being a big fish in this small pond?''

''If you want to put it that way—yes,'' Davidson said.

''Whilst you remain our keepers—the men with the nets, with the power of removing and destroying any one of us at any time?''

''You're being deliberately obtuse,'' Davidson said angrily.

''From your standpoint possibly,'' Gerry said. ''It's really a matter of point of view, isn't it?''

Davidson was about to reply when a hum coursed through the semispherical entry point. Both of them turned, to see that a red light had flashed into life above the elevator door.

''This will be Ulanov and Meyer now,'' Davidson said. ''Now I want you to remember that, whatever natural hostility you may feel towards this man, it has no foundation in true reality.''

''The meeting of the two educated Pinocchios,'' Gerry said, grinning.

The grin faded as the door of the elevator hissed open to reveal not two occupants, but one; a tall woman in a black cat-suit, who was—*incredibly*—Kay. Kay, whose dreadfully mutilated remains he had left in the fire-ravaged remains of the shelter. Kay, whom he had loved, and for whom he had grieved so long. Transfixed by shock, he remained staring silently as the woman stepped from the elevator, her attention on Davidson.

''Laura! What happened? Where is Ulanov?''

111

"Gorst broke in while I was Reprogramming him."

"Gorst? But where in hell was Meyer?" demanded Davidson.

"He did his best, but he wasn't able to stop Gorst smashing the Senso-taper."

"And Ulanov?"

"He was half-way through programming," Laura said. "The destruction of the Senso-taper left him in a state of traumatic shock. The only thing I could do was to shoot him full of anaesthetic and leave him there. Gorst too, and another man. We shall have to get a pickup squad to take them out before daylight. In the meantime Meyer will have to remain in charge of the Southern Sector."

"You think he's capable?"

"Not really, he's liable to crack up under the first bit of added strain—but what else could I do? I had to come and tell you what had happened."

"Yes . . . of course. I'd better get up there and see if I can put some backbone into him," Davidson said. "We may still be able to pull it off, if the guerillas will accept his leadership. I'll call Control first, and arrange for the pickup squad." Completely preoccupied, he hurried across to the vidphone on the wall a couple of meters from the elevator.

"You must be Clyne," the woman said, turning her light-brown eyes on Gerry for the first time. "I've seen you on the monitors, of course." She stepped forward and offered her hand. "I'm Laura Frayne."

Gerry took the hand, looking into the dark greasepaint-smeared features, wondering if the hair beneath the black cap she wore was, as he suspected, honey-blonde. It was impossible, a reincarnation . . . He wanted to say: "No—you're not Laura Frayne, you're Kay Linder, and I love you." Instead, he remained silent, feeling the warm vitality of the hand in his grasp.

At last, she removed the hand gently, a nervous smile tugging at the corners of her mouth as she said: "Strange, somehow I'd expected you to be louder, more brash."

Gerry laughed, releasing some of the tension within him. "I'm sorry if I'm a disappointment. It's just that you remind me very strongly of someone I used to know. Or did I?

112

Maybe you're just something that Davidson fed into my mind when he was Programming me.''

She looked across at Davidson, who was still talking into the vidphone. "That's possible," she said quietly, her fine features hardening. "Later, we shall have to do something about it."

"No," Gerry said. "This business of having two complete sets of memories can be confusing, but I'd rather keep my mind the way it is from now on."

Davidson turned from the vidphone and approached them. His lean face was very pale. "Damn that Pelissier! Why does he always have to make everything so difficult?"

"He's sending a squad?" Laura asked.

"Yes, but the way he makes it sound, I'm asking him a personal favor."

"You'll have to go easy on Avram Meyer. He's had about as much as he can take," Laura said. "He really should be got out of the environment right away."

"Impossible!" Davidson said. "We need him Inside, if we're to maintain control over the guerilla sector."

"And the north?"

"Clyne understands the situation. He can handle things there."

Laura frowned. "Even so, I think I should go back with him."

"That's not necessary," Davidson snapped. "In any case, I may need you."

"Aren't you forgetting about Torrance?" Laura said. "Once he realizes what is happening, he's sure to give trouble. I should be there."

Davidson hesitated, his eyes flickering from one to the other of the man and woman who faced him. "Oh, very well," he said at length. "I can't stay here arguing with you. God knows what Meyer may be up to. Go back with Clyne, if you like—but keep in touch by radio. Now I must be going."

He hurried into the elevator, and the doors hissed shut behind him.

As the hum of the ascending elevator faded, Gerry turned to Laura. "What kind of a group is it that gets itself a leader like him?" he asked.

Laura reacted defensively. "Michael has been under strain. The circumstances . . ."

"Strain, hell!" Gerry said. "He's as neurotic as a panicking rabbit, running in all directions at once."

"Whereas you, I take it, are a model of stability?" Laura said coolly.

Clyne grinned. "I asked for that, criticizing your Messiah, didn't I?"

"Michael is a very sincere person. He has been disturbed about the situation Inside for a long time."

"And you?"

"Do you really imagine that any woman could be complacent about the suffering that has been going on in here?"

"Possibly not, but hasn't it ever occurred to you that suffering and violence may be a necessary part of life?"

"Human beings should be able to live in peace together."

"No conflicts, just a nice, quiet stagnation—is that the idea? With your training, you can still believe that?"

She faced him stiffly, with an arrogant femininity that he found irresistibly attractive.

"You talk like Moule."

"The director of the project? Well, could be that he's right, after all. Look at this plan of yours. It was all very fine in theory for Davidson to preach his gospel of nonviolence, but it hasn't worked out that way so far, has it? Maybe you made a mistake in coming into conflict with your own established authority?"

"Moule's policy is wrong. Many have felt that for a long time, but Michael's ideas crystallized our thinking into action."

"Then Moule must be an idiot to allow such a thing to happen. He should have got rid of Davidson as soon as he started to open his mouth."

"He tried. Michael was going to be shipped back to Earth tomorrow."

"I see." The reason for Davidson's agitation became evident to Gerry now. The plan might have been in preparation for some time, but it had been pushed forward, hurried into action because of this happening. "And now, do you really think Moule is going to back down so easily?"

114

"What else can he do?"

"Surely he could ask for help from Earth to back his policy?"

"No—once things have been changed Inside, it would be too much of an upheaval to reestablish them as they were. Faced by a *fait accompli*, Moule can do no other than accept the situation."

Gerry laughed. "You and Davidson—you've got it all worked out, haven't you? Inside is going to be turned into some kind of Arcadia, with everybody happy and contented, enjoying themselves, whether they like it or not. And me —what have you in mind for me? Erasure and Reconditioning, perhaps?"

She stared at him, genuinely shocked. "Why do you say that?"

He shrugged. "Well, I'm hardly the type to fit in with the Arcadian concept. I've never been very good at passive contentment, or hadn't you guessed?"

"There's no such plan, I assure you."

"No?" Gerry said. "Maybe Davidson just hasn't told you, eh? Sure, I'm useful to him at the moment, but later on he may decide that my knowledge of the true situation constitutes a potential danger. Then what?"

"I think it's time we were going," she said, moving ahead of him towards the waiting vehicle.

Gerry watched the grace of her movements for a moment, then followed. He found himself wondering why Davidson had put her into his Programming, and just how and why he had manufactured the memories that were still clear in his mind of his relationship-that-never-was with Kay/Laura. However it had been done, it had been done so well that despite his knowledge of the falsity of those memories, he was more than half in love with this woman. At the same time he found himself wondering if it was also due to his programming that he had this extraordinary conviction that she felt at least an equal attraction towards him.

CHAPTER EIGHTEEN

They talked in a matter-of-fact manner as she drove the runabout towards the Northern Sector, and she answered his questions about the underground network and the manner in which the Control Dome was run, although it occurred to her that Davidson might have been disapproving of her openness in such matters. Despite an outward show of cooperation with Clyne, it was quite obvious to her that for some reason she did not understand, Michael disliked and distrusted the man, and was only using him as a means to an end. Possibly part of the reason for Michael's attitude was the fact that this big, smiling man who sat close beside her in the small vehicle, seemingly completely relaxed, was in direct contrast to his own bony neuroticism.

Most of the time she used the excuse of concentrating on her steering to avoid looking directly into Clyne's face, but despite this she found herself increasingly aware of the powerful maleness that surrounded him like an aura. There was arrogance there, but at the same time there was gentleness and humor. On the few times she did allow herself to look directly into his eyes, it was to find there an electrifying frankness that seemed to pierce down through all her reserve in its naked appeal to her femininity. She knew somehow that this was a real man, who was capable of bringing her to a new consciousness of her womanhood; a man who would dominate her, but at the same time complement her in a way no other ever had. Somewhere she had read that if there was such a thing as male beauty, its main ingredient must be vitality, but until this moment she had not appreciated the full significance of the definition. Despite her self-mocking efforts to shake off the conviction by telling herself that she was reacting like a fifteen-year-old virgin, it seemed to her that Gerry Clyne was the most beautiful, desirable man she had ever met.

A gray dawn light was beginning to filter through the dome

as they left the power station entry point. They walked through the deserted streets of the Northern Sector, and even though they were not so physically close now as they had been in the runabout, she found herself more conscious than ever of the arrogant maleness of his body, of the smooth controlled strength of each movement.

"You must be tired," he said.

"It has been a long night," she admitted. "Where are we going?"

"Back to my place for a shower, and some coffee. We'll both feel better for it."

"Sounds a good idea. And then?"

"Then we'd better have a few words with your friend Torrance," he said.

"Yes, I suppose you're right." It was an encounter that she was not anticipating with pleasure. Torrance had always been of an independent nature. It was quite possible that even though he was faced by an already changed situation Inside, he would refuse to bow to the inevitable. In that case she would be forced to use the hypo gun which hung in its place at her waist belt—but the thought of performing such an act on Torrance was somehow distasteful to her, carrying with it implications of treachery which left her with a deep feeling of discomfort.

There was a quality of uncluttered neatness about the interior of Clyne's bungalow that made it seem like an extension of his personality. He was that kind of man—one who would leave his mark on anything he touched, changing it in some way by the very force of his own aliveness.

He led her into the small, well-equipped kitchen. "Coffee? And what about food? Ham and eggs?"

"Just coffee, I think."

He grinned. "Nonsense! You must be hungry, and if you aren't you will be by the time you've had a shower." He walked over and opened the door of the compact bathroom. "You go ahead. I'll just have a quick swill at the sink, and then get on with breakfast."

Inside the bathroom she stood for a moment looking at her reflection in the wall mirror. Her hair when she removed the black cap was tousled and strawlike, and the black makeup

117

on her face had run in places, giving a zebralike effect. God! what a fright she looked. How could she have ever imagined that Clyne would find her attractive in such a state? She peeled off the grimy cat-suit and switched on the shower.

The water was delightfully hot and inviting, and she was soaping herself over for the second time when she became aware that she was not alone in the bathroom. She turned.

He was standing smiling, watching her.

"Well, do you approve?" she said, as his eyes finally finished their leisurely survey of her body and returned to meet her own.

"Let's say I just changed my mind about breakfast," he said, unbuttoning his shirt with precise, unhurried movements.

She awoke, jerking upright in a sudden panic of disorientation at the strangeness of the room, then relaxed again as she remembered where she was. It had been good—better than anything she had ever experienced before. But somehow she had known it would be that way, from the first moment of their meeting. He had made love with a ruthless, searching eroticism that raised her to undreamed-of heights of passion, and now as she lay there the echoes of that pattern reverberated through her body, and she wanted him again—again, and forever, because his was the masculinity she had been made to enfold, to cherish within her being.

She looked at the clock on the wall opposite and realized that she had been asleep for over three hours. With a qualm of guilt, she recalled that her personal radio must still be in the bathroom with her discarded clothes. Had Davidson been trying to contact her? If not, he would have expected to receive at least a checking call before this time. Lazily, she raised herself to a sitting position. Somehow it didn't seem important any more, not beside what had happened, but . . .

The sound of the bungalow's front door opening interrupted her thoughts. She listened to the approaching footsteps, then a moment later, he stood in the doorway of the bedroom.

"Where have you been?" she asked.

"There were arrangements to be made." His face was strangely opaque, changed.

"Torrance?"

"He's under guard. There will be no difficulty there."

"And now?" There was something different about him—a new tension had taken the place of the casual relaxed manner. She wanted to understand the reason for the change, and at the same time she feared what she might discover.

"I need your help," he said.

"Help—in what?"

He moved across the room and stood about a meter away, looking down at her. There were hard lines at the corners of his mouth and eyes that she had not noticed before. "There will be a hundred men at the power station in an hour. We could find our own way, but it will save time if you come along and guide us through the underground."

"But there's no need. I'll admit that the underground would be an ideal way of approaching the guerrilla camp for a surprise attack, but the war is over. Davidson has promised . . ." Her voice trailed away as she recalled that she was talking merely to conceal meaning.

"The guerillas are no longer of any importance," he said, shaking his head. "Our objective is the Control Dome."

She stared at him, the bluntness of his statement leaving her temporarily speechless. And yet, even on their short acquaintance she was able to understand that this plan was totally in keeping with the ruthless, uncompromising nature of the man.

"You didn't really think I would be prepared to settle for anything less, did you?" he said. "Since none of us Inside is supposed to know of the existence of the underground, or of the Control Dome itself, for that matter—I suspect that there will be little in the way of defenses. And even if there are, the monitoring blackout arranged by Davidson will provide us with ideal cover. That is why we must strike quickly, with or without your help. But if you do come along, it may help save lives and unnecessary bloodshed."

She began to tremble as the full impact of his words filtered through her mind. "You bastard! You conniving, utterly ruthless bastard!'' she said. ''So that was the reason you played the great lover.''

He returned her gaze steadily. ''If you want to believe that, you can. But you'd be selling yourself short.''

She was off the bed now, the fact of her nakedness unimportant as she stood facing him clothed in the armor of rage. ''What else can I believe? I should have known from the beginning, even when I let you . . . use me.''

''You're making confused, emotional judgments,'' he said quietly. ''We *used* each other, if you want to put it that way, because of the biochemical reaction, not because of who, or what, either of us was. It was a man/woman thing, on a completely different level.''

Although she knew instinctively that there was some truth in what he said, her pride made it impossible to accept. ''And you really think that because of this . . . relationship, I should be prepared to betray my colleagues in Control, and ruin the plan?''

''The *plan*!'' He rejected the word contemptuously. ''You said yourself that its success was based on the idea of two strong leaders Inside, leaders capable of coming to logical agreement between themselves, and enforcing the observance of peace on their followers. I could do that in this sector, and Ulanov would have been capable of doing so with the guerillas. But not Meyer—not without telling them the whole truth, and Davidson will not allow him to do that.''

''But you have told your people?''

He nodded. ''What did you expect? Did you really believe, like that idealistic fool Davidson, that you could hand a prisoner the key to his cage, and at the same time put him on his honor not to use it? Did you think that, knowing what I now know, I would be prepared to go on playing Davidson's game, reorganizing Inside into some kind of Arcadia to salve *his* conscience? Could you possibly imagine that I would be prepared to accept such a role, in the full knowledge that Davidson and others like him would go on forever monitoring my every action? The very idea is an obscenity.''

She felt the raw edge of his disgust as he flung the questions at her without pause, and despite the fact that what he was saying went against all her conditioning, she could see the validity of his arguments.

"I'll grant you that the idea of constant surveillance is in itself a denial of human dignity," she began, but he interrupted her.

"Human dignity? You dare to talk to me of that, when the mind of each one of us in here has been probed and manipulated by Davidson and the rest of them, so that we are forced to spend our time in here fighting like animals amongst ourselves for totally false reasons?"

"You already know what I, what most of us, feel about that," she protested, on the defensive now. "It was Moule's policy, not ours—a policy which we were determined to change."

"To replace it with yet another false reality?" His right hand made a gesture of dismissal. "I spit on your reality!"

"But what else *could* we do?"

"You could have told us the truth."

"To what purpose? This truth of yours is like a corrosive, ever-expanding gas, eating away at the foundations of rationality. Now that you know what you are, and why you are here—does that make you any more content?"

"Content—what is *content*?" he demanded. "If that was all we needed, then surely it would have been simpler to lobotomize us all and turn us into placid vegetables. At least Moule rejected that alternative."

"Then perhaps the war with the guerillas was not so pointless after all," she suggested. "At least it channelled off your aggressive impulses in a comparatively harmless manner. What you are proposing now is something a great deal more serious."

"From your point of view—or ours?"

"What can you possibly hope to gain by invading the Control Dome?" she asked. "After all, it's only another dome like this one, but smaller. Even if you do succeed in taking it over, all you will have done is to increase the size of your prison. There can still be no real escape. Where would you escape to? Certainly not back to an Earth that has already rejected you."

"At least when we have the Control Dome there will be no more surveillance."

"And what about the people now working in Control?"

"If they show themselves willing to cooperate, they will be integrated into our new society."

"And if not?"

"Then they will have to be . . . adjusted."

"Why not say what you really mean—that they will be Reprogrammed?" she said. "You're just going to replace one kind of tyranny with another. Now you will be the masters—is that the idea?"

"We are the majority," he pointed out.

"Agreed, but what makes you so sure you're right?"

He stepped forward, grasping her naked shoulders with a gentle firmness, as he looked deep into her eyes. "Because I have to be—don't you see?" he said intensely. "The situation is changed now. Davidson changed it, for better or for worse, when he gave me back my true memories. There can be no going back."

Perhaps it had been an accident of biochemistry in the first instance, but now, above all else, she found herself wanting to believe in this man, because without him life could have no meaning. "You promise that there will be no killing?" she said.

"Not if it can be avoided," he said. "But remember that, if you don't come with us, we may be forced to defend ourselves."

She weighed the situation in her mind. There was little doubt that, with or without her help, he would take over the Control Dome. There were, as he had guessed, no real defenses against invasion through the underground; certainly none that would stand against his force and determination. On the face of it, by aiding him she would be a traitor to her own colleagues, but if by being that she helped to save their lives . . .

"The future," she said. "What happens after you have taken over the Control Dome?"

"We live—but all of us in the same reality. Those who don't wish to stay can go back to Earth on the supply ship."

She frowned. "If there *is* a supply ship."

"Earth will not starve us out, if that's what you're thinking," he said. "Now that we're not preoccupied with that stupid war, we shall be able to produce sufficient food for both domes."

"But how can you be sure that they will stand placidly by and . . ."

"And watch the patients take over the asylum?" he grinned suddenly. "Baby, I've got news for you, there's not a damned thing Earth can do about it. That will be my first message to them."

"And the function of the Mars project as a safety valve for Earth. Somewhere to syphon off the psychotics and malcontents?"

"I shall tell them that if they still need a safety valve, they can go on sending us people. Didn't you know that Australia was once a penal colony? And they haven't done so badly."

It was as much due to the hypnotic power of his self-confidence as to her feelings for him as a man that she found herself understanding that what he said made sense to her—more sense than the previous situation on Mars, with its two, deliberately compartmented realities. The patients *were* about to take over the asylum, but with a leader like Gerry Clyne in command and the cooperation of the specialists in the Control Dome . . .

"All right," she said. "I'll help you."

"That's fine . . . fine," he said. He pulled her gently towards him and kissed her.

As she gave herself to the pleasure it occurred to her that he had deliberately waited for her decision before surrendering to the impulse. Perhaps even Gerry Clyne could be tamed in time. It was an interesting thought.

CHAPTER NINETEEN

The pickup squad had gone, leaving Davidson and Meyer alone together in the guerilla headquarters. Meyer sat slumped in a chair, the paleness of his haggard face accentuated by his jet-black hair. At times he seemed to be unaware of Davidson's presence, sunk deep in a morass of hopelessness.

Davidson's impatience was growing, as he tried to batter his way through the other's lethargy. "I fail to see where the difficulty lies," he said. "You are recognized as Ulanov's second-in-command. All you need do is to tell the men that he and Gorst have gone off on a secret mission, leaving you in charge until they come back."

"And the disappearance of the sentry?" Avram Meyer's deep-brown eyes turned on him mournfully.

"Damn it, man! You're making difficulties," snapped Davidson. "The sentry is unimportant. You can say that he went with them."

"All right, so I tell them that. But when none of the three comes back, what then? The men will expect me to send out scouting parties looking for them at least. More than that, they will expect reprisals against the Northern Sector."

"There must be no reprisals," Davidson said. "Don't you understand? The war is over. There will be no more fighting Inside."

"Of course I understand—but how am I to convince the men that the war is suddenly over without presenting them with some believable reason for this being so? Even Ulanov would find it difficult to put such a proposition to them—they certainly won't accept it from me. Without Ulanov's backing, they'll think I've sold out, surrendered. I shall have a mutiny on my hands."

"Not if you handle it in the right way," argued Davidson. "Good God man, do you imagine that these men—that *any* men—want to go on forever fighting this kind of war?"

Meyer showed some sign of animation. "Yes—in their case, I think that may well be so. It might be different if they had some idea of returning to their homes at the end of the war, but they know that is impossible. The continuance of this conflict is the only thing that gives their lives any meaning, can't you see that?"

Davidson sighed his frustration. The trouble was that, in many respects, he knew that Meyer's analysis of the situation was correct. Meyer had originally been choosen for this particular role because his negative, self-effacing personality made him a suitable foil for the dominating Ulanov. It was argued that such a man was less likely to clash with the fiery colonel, and would thus be a more efficient observer. No one had anticipated the present, changed circumstances, which had thrust Meyer into the position of leader and changed what had previously been assets into liabilities.

"All right, then we shall have to play it this way," Davidson said. "Suppose you tell the men this story about Ulanov and Gorst having gone on a mission, and explain that any attack might prejudice the success of that mission."

"And how long do you think they're going to be content with that?" said Meyer.

"At least you should be able to hold them for two or three days," Davidson said. "Time enough for me to Reprogram both Ulanov and Gorst. After that, the two of them will be delivered back here, equipped with a complete set of memories rationalizing the new, peace situation, which they will naturally pass on to the men."

"Yes, I suppose that might work," Meyer said, without enthusiasm.

Davidson wheeled on him angrily. "So what's bugging you now?" he demanded.

"I was talking to Laura Frayne earlier," Meyer said. "She said there was a chance of my being relieved quite soon. God! To live in a sane society again . . ."

"You'll be relieved," Davidson said. "But first we must stabilize the situation Inside." He walked across to the window and looked out. It was now full daylight outside, and all chance of getting back to the underground entrance point unseen was gone. "I shall have to wait here until tonight. Do you think you can manage to make sure that nobody comes into the back room?"

Without waiting for Meyer's reply, he walked into the sleeping quarters and closed the door behind him. Taking out his miniaturized radio transceiver, he called Hofer in the Control Dome. The electronics man told him that everything was going smoothly there so far, but pointed out that Moule would not be expecting his first reports from Monitor Section for a couple of hours yet. When those failed to arrive, there

125

would have to be some explanation for the apparent major failure in the surveillance system.

It had been Davidson's original plan to confront Moule personally with the changed situation Inside before the resumption of monitoring, but his temporary confinement here in the guerilla sector made it necessary to abandon that idea. Hofer seemed hopeful about his ability to stall in the matter of repairs to the monitoring network, but even so, Moule must surely guess that something unusual was going on. Under the circumstances, the prospect of a whole day's enforced inactivity was maddening. It seemed that apart from checking on the progress of Clyne and Laura Frayne in the Northern Sector, there was little else he could do but wait for nightfall. At least there was little doubt about the ability of those two to handle the situation there, although he did have some qualms about the possible development of their personal relationship. He had not intended in the first instance that they should meet at all face to face, but there again events had not worked out according to plan.

After giving Hofer instructions to pass onto the other members of the group, he broke contact and pushed the selector button on his transceiver to call Laura Frayne.

A couple of minutes later, apart from a crackle of background static, the receiver still remained mute. He tried again.

There was still no reply.

Davidson began to pace the floor of the small room uneasily, wondering about the possible reasons for Laura's lack of response. When he had left her in the underground with Clyne the transceiver had been in its place, hooked at her belt, where she could hardly ignore its demanding "beep." If she was physically capable of doing so, it was inconceivable that Laura would ignore his call. She was an experienced operator, aware of the importance of maintaining communications in such a situation.

He tried again, but the result was the same. Nothing but the negative hiss of static. Apprehension growing, he checked through the possible reasons for Laura's lack of response. It could be that her transceiver had developed some freak fault, or his own, even . . .

126

He called Hofer again, and instructed the electronics specialist to try and raise Laura with his more powerful transmitter.

Several minutes later his own receiver beeped. He switched on.

"Nothing there, Mike," Hofer said. "You're sure she was carrying her radio?"

"Of course I'm sure," Davidson snapped.

"In that case, something must have happened to her," Hofer said. "You want me to send someone into the Northern Sector to trace her?"

Davidson came to a sudden decision. "No—I'll handle this myself," he said.

"But Mike . . ."

"I'll call you back within the hour," Davidson said, cutting off Hofer's protestations. He moved to the door. opening it gently, he saw that Meyer was standing alone by the map table, his pale face brooding.

"Meyer, I've got to get out of here now!"

Meyer turned to face him. "But that's impossible. It's broad daylight."

"Then we've got to make it possible. I can't make contact with Laura by radio, so I have to get to the Northern Sector and find out what's happened to her."

"But how? You may be seen."

"You'll have to escort me. If we meet any of your men, you can tell them that I'm a prisoner whom you're interrogating."

"But . . ."

"No *buts*, Meyer," Davidson cut in harshly. "Just do as I say. Now, let's get moving."

CHAPTER TWENTY

Private Sikorski squatted beneath the tree on the edge of the clearing, listening to the rumblings of his belly and cursing the stupidity of his superiors, who insisted on playing everything strictly according to the book. Guard duty out here, to the south of the camp, was a complete waste of time. Everyone knew that this was a dead sector, that the northerners wouldn't attack here, if they attacked at all—so why bother?

Sikorski lolled against the mossy trunk and winced as his shoulder pack rubbed against the still-tender flesh of his back. Thirty lashes . . . for doing something that was only natural for a man. Gorst and Ulanov—those stiff-necked bastards with their pious talk about crimes against a woman prisoner. Gorst got his share, that was for sure, and Ulanov didn't lead quite the monk's life he pretended. But in this man's army it was always the old story from the officers and the non-coms: "Do as I say, not as I do"—and it was Ivan, the private, who took the kicks and the punishments when he stepped out of line.

"Bastards, stiff-necked bastards!" muttered Sikorski, his right hand tightening round the butt of his automatic rifle as he recalled the way Gorst had stood by, barking out the count as the lashes seared down on his bare back—and how the warrant officer had counted twenty-nine three times, and nobody had dared question.

Remembering the whistle of the thongs through the air and the biting, white-hot pain of flayed flesh, Sikorski thought: *One of these days there'll be just Gorst and me, out there somewhere on a raid together, parted from the others in the squad. Just half a minute, that's all I'll need; time to see Gorst's eyes as I squeeze the trigger. He has to know it's me, otherwise it won't be right. I've got to see the panic, the pleading in his eyes, as the stream of bullets cuts him in half.*

And afterwards . . . The explanation would be easy. We stumbled into an ambush, and Gorst, who was in front—he was always in front—took the first burst of fire. Things like that happened all the time in this kind of warfare, and there wouldn't be too many questions, even if someone was shot in the back . . .

But the back is no good—I've got to see that look—the fear in his eyes. I won't have the satisfaction of telling anybody afterwards—although there are some who may guess—but that won't matter so much if I get those few seconds when he

128

and I know. When he looks at me, and realizes that I'm going to kill him. That will be the real satisfaction.

Ivan Sikorski lolled sleepily beneath the bush, his ruddy, peasant face set in a grin of anticipation as he dreamed his dream of vengeance on Gorst for those extra lashes.

How do you like half a hundred bullets in your fat gut, Comrade Warrant Officer?

The dream faded suddenly as somewhere, not very far away, a footstep crackled on brittle undergrowth. Soldier's senses immediately alert, Sikorski eased himself behind the tree, the automatic rifle dropping to the ready position. He glanced at his watch. Still three-quarters of an hour to go before he was due to be relieved. Who then was the intruder? Was it the platoon sergeant making a surprise check, in the hope of finding someone asleep on duty? Another thirty lashes, at least, for that crime.

Or was it a raid from the Northern Sector? No, not here. This was the least likely place for them to strike. And yet . . . The mind of Sikorski abandoned its private fantasies, reacting with the alertness ingrained by years of military training.

Footsteps were coming closer now, clumsily crackling and swishing through the vegetation. Surely no raiding party could be so careless of revealing its presence—unless on the assumption that this sector could not possibly be guarded.

There were voices now. Two men, talking quietly together. Sikorski stiffened. One of the voices was vaguely familiar, and the other had a strange, foreign accent that he recognized. It was the same kind of accent the woman had had, when she cursed and struggled—the accent of the north.

Two men appeared at the far side of the clearing. The identity of one of them was immediately apparent, linking as it did with the sound of his voice, it could be none other that Comrade Captain Meyer. But the other . . .

A tall, thin stranger, wearing a close-fitting black suit, and talking with a foreign accent. A northern spy! What else could he be? And with Captain Meyer. All officers were pigs—could it be that this one was also a traitor?

Resisting the temptation to leap out and challenge the two men, Sikorski remained where he was, watching as they skirted the edge of the clearing and stopped by the stump of a

129

felled tree. Curiosity prickled at the back of his neck as he saw the foreigner remove a small, penlike object from his belt, and point it at the tree stump. A few seconds later, driven by silent, unseen power, the huge stump began to move sideways and upwards, like a hinged lid, revealing some kind of manhole.

The black-suited foreigner was already stepping down into the hole when Sikorski launched himself forward out of his hiding place.

"Halt!"

At the sound of Sikorski's shout, Meyer's hand flew to his sidearm holster, his body turning to face the challenge. Behind him, the foreigner looked up in alarm.

Reflexively, faced by a man about to draw a weapon, Sikorski's finger squeezed the trigger of his automatic rifle. A brief burst of bullets patterned neatly in the heart area of Meyer's chest. His pale face frozen in a curiously vacuous expression of surprise, the captain tottered sideways, temporarily hiding the figure of the foreigner.

By the time his body had hit the ground, the black-suited figure had disappeared. Sikorski stood, hearing the distant whistles of other guards, knowing that help would be to hand within a minute or so. Meanwhile, conscious of his exposed position, he crouched with his weapon at the ready, and began to stalk carefully forward towards the hinged tree stump.

Five meters . . . four . . . His hands on the weapon were clammy with sweat, his eyes searching for the other man.

"Come out with your hands up!" His voice was harsh, unnatural, forced from a fear-constricted throat.

Silence, except for the distant sounds of feet in the undergrowth, his comrades approaching. Sikorski moved closer to the crumpled form of Meyer. A pig of an officer, not so bad as Ulanov, perhaps, but a pig—and he was dead, rot him.

The sharp crack of a single report.

Ivan Sikorski, a bullet hole drilled neatly between his eyes, fell forward, his broad face burying itself in the lush grass of the clearing.

The black-suited figure appeared again from behind the

130

upturned tree stump. Grasping the limp body of Meyer beneath the shoulders, it lugged the burden towards the exposed manhole and disappeared beneath the ground.

A moment later, the tree stump moved soundlessly back into its original position, leaving the body of Private Ivan Sikorski alone in the clearing.

CHAPTER TWENTY-ONE

Davidson propped the limp body against the wall of the underground entrance point. His hands felt sticky, and looking down he saw that they were red with Meyer's blood. The sight brought on a violent, trembling nausea. He had watched the fighting Inside many times on Control monitor screens, but death, immediate and bloody, had been until this moment quite outside his experience.

He bent down and wiped his hands as best he could on Meyer's clothing. Strange irony that this should have happened to Meyer, who had been so afraid. Could it be that his fear had not really been cowardice, but the result of some overwhelming precognition of the fate that awaited him? The fear was gone now. The pale face held no expression at all—just a complete blankness.

Blankness . . . the thought reminded him of his obligation to Meyer. It was part of standing instructions to Control personnel that all fatalities should be returned for revivification and surgery at the earliest possible moment, in order to minimize deterioration of the brain cells. His anxieties about Laura would have to wait for the time being. Under the circumstances, it was his unequivocal duty to supervise personally the return of Meyer's body to Control before doing anything else. Apart from that, it was now more important than ever that Ulanov and Gorst should be Reprogrammed and returned Inside at the earliest possible moment—and this was a task that only he could perform with the degree of efficiency required.

He hurried across to the vid and called Transport, who assured him that a vehicle would be despatched to collect himself and Meyer immediately.

Meyer was sitting there in a pool of his own blood, his face, slumped towards his ruined chest, had a greenish-gray pallor. Poor devil! Personnel had made a mistake in selecting him for this kind of work in the first place. He just hadn't been the type. Still, he was out of it now. Boehm and the others would mend his bones, supply him with new organs and blood, and the death-trauma would be carefully erased from his Psyche-profile. He would be confused and shaky at first, but eventually he would be all right, capable of taking on some other job in Control, or if he wished, being returned to Earth and invalided out of his contract. Maybe it was the best thing for him after all. He had certainly not been happy in his work as a Role-Player. There was no denying the truth of Laura's opinion in that matter.

Laura . . . The thought reminded him that he had not tried to call her for some time. He punched the selector button on his transceiver.

The response was almost immediate. "Frayne here."

"Laura! Where the devil have you been? I've been trying to get you for hours."

There was a slight hesitation before she replied. "Sorry, Mike. I had to keep my receiver switched off. Couldn't risk being called when I was in the middle of a bunch of Insiders. They were suspicious enough of me as it was."

Davidson frowned. The excuse made some sense, of course. In fact, he might have guessed if he had been thinking straight that this was the reason for her lack of reply. The unwelcome thought came to him that if he had come to such a conclusion earlier, then Meyer might still have been alive.

Thrusting aside the self-questioning doubts, he said: "What's happening there?"

"All going smoothly. How's Avram?"

"He'll be O.K. I'm on my way back to Control, to supervise the Reprogramming of Ulanov," Davidson said. There was no point in alarming Laura with the story of Meyer's death at this stage. He suspected that her degree of personal involvement with the man might cause some distraction from her task of keeping tabs on Clyne.

"You're going to put Ulanov and Gorst in again?"

"Better that way. Meyer isn't strong enough to handle the situation here."

"I'm sure you're right about that," Laura said. "I was going to recommend his relief at the earliest possible moment."

Davidson heard the hum of an approaching vehicle. "That sounds like my transport coming," he said. "I'll sign off now, and you can call me at Control in an hour's time, if you've anything to report."

"Will do," Laura said, and broke contact.

Davidson turned as the vehicle rolled to a halt and one of Pelissier's men stepped out of the driving seat.

"Hell! That looks like a messy one," said the driver, looking down at the sprawling, blood-sodden body of Meyer.

CHAPTER TWENTY-TWO

"I mean, let's face it, all us G.D. homies could just as well be doing the same kinda job back on Earth. I mean, what am I but a truck-driver, when you come down to it? Those Role-Players, they're the boys who get the glamour and the action, even if they do end up getting themselves stiffed now and again. Still, what's that these days? I mean, no time at all they'll have him patched up and walking around again . . ."

Seated beside the tediously talkative driver the journey back to the main terminus of the underground, which lay directly below the Control Dome, seemed to take longer than normal. Davidson let the monologue rattle on and on, turning from time to time to look back at the vehicle's cargo, the waxen-faced, bloody mess that had been Avram Meyer. He had never liked the man particularly, or had a great deal of respect for him, but he must have had some kind of special courage to make him volunteer for that kind of work in the first instance. Or perhaps he was really a coward, deliberately overcompensating to prove something to himself? Whichever was the truth, it was unimportant beside the fact of that inert, stiffening body, and Davidson was uncomfortably aware of the fact that if it hadn't been for his own insistence on going back to the underground entry point in broad daylight Meyer would still have been alive.

Boehm and the surgeons would revive him, and replace the irreparable organs, but what then? What did you say to a man who had been killed because of your own thoughtless action? What was it like to have been dead, and then revived? Even though his death would only be temporary, looking at Meyer's blank-faced corpse the condition seemed to have a terrible finality that no amount of surgical skill could possibly nullify. Meyer would be reprogrammed, the traumatic death experience erased from his brain, but something must surely remain, if only on an unconscious level, and as far as Davidson was concerned the man's presence could only offer accusation of his own guilt.

". . . some of these so-called experts aren't so darned clever when you get down to it," the driver continued. "I mean, like this business of the entire monitoring system being out of whack now for going on twelve hours. Holy jumping Christ—I get a burned out coil, or something, and Pelissier bawls me out like I'd sabotaged the whole goddamned solar system. But Hofer and his crowd of eggheads, all they got to do is make some kinda mouth noises about technical faults and nobody gives them a hard time. So like it seems you got to be an expert to get away with making a cock-up of your job. Say, that reminds me—you hear the one about the Programmer who got himself linked into a feedback circuit with a hermaphrodite? It seems there was . . ."

Davidson focused on the blank gray walls of the corridor, resisting the temptation to look back yet again at the cargo. There was nothing, nothing at all that he personally could do for Meyer at this stage—neither was there any point in torturing himself with guilt feelings. There would be a great deal to be done, when he arrived back in the Control Dome. Hofer and the others were apparently carrying out their agreed tasks with reasonable efficiency—but it was he, as their acknowledged leader, who had to perform the two crucial tasks—first of leading the group that would confront Moule, and tell him that he had been deposed from his directorship—and second, of talking to the entire population of the Control Dome over the public address system and convincing them that it was in their own interest to cooperate with the new regime.

And Moule—how would he take it? In a way, Davidson found himself hoping—badly. Not that he wanted to do physical violence to the man—but there would be some satisfaction in seeing that proud ugliness humbled, that stolid confidence broken down at last.

". . . and so the herma said, 'Yes, that's all very well, but how does my sister fit into this?' " The driver delivered the punchline of the long, involved joke at last, almost rolling out of his seat in appreciation of his own wit as he steered the vehicle into the gleaming terminus of Control Central. "Looks like your reception party," he said, as he pulled to a halt near a couple of medical orderlies who were waiting with an empty stretcher trolley.

Davidson stepped to the ground as soon as the vehicle was stationary, and after a brief word with the orderlies, he hurried towards the Transport Controller's office.

Pelissier looked up, his pink, patrician features showing a curious expression of strain as Davidson barged unceremoniously into the inner office.

"You took your time sending that moron of a driver," Davidson said. "Don't you realize everything depends on our getting this whole thing wrapped up before the supply ship arrives?"

"In that case you would have been better to have remained here in Control, rather than trotting about Inside trying to play the one-man superhero, wouldn't you?" Pelissier said sharply.

"It was necessary that I should activate Clyne—after all, I programmed him," Davidson said, puzzled by the other's near-hysterical tone, and the obvious air of tension that surrounded him.

"You could equally well have programmed him so that

someone else could have provided the trigger stimulus,"
Pelissier said. "How long do you think I would be able to
keep this section running if I insisted on tightening every nut
and checking every meter reading personally. Delegation is
the only solution, under such circumstances. But you can't
accept that, can you?"

"What's wrong, Pelissier?" asked Davidson, his own
sense of alarm growing in response to the transport chief's
ill-suppressed agitation.

"Wrong? Nothing's wrong," Pelissier snapped. "It's just
that I still think the whole thing has been too rushed. We
should have taken more time, and made sure of our ground
with the rank and file workers."

"They'll follow once we've got Moule in the bag,"
Davidson said. "Where is he now, anyway?"

"In his office, as far as I know."

"Good!" Davidson pointed to the desk vid. "Call the
others and tell them to meet me in twenty minutes in the
Programming Section."

"There won't be any need for that, Davidson," said a
voice behind him.

He whirled, to see the familiar, bearlike figure of Torrance
standing in the open doorway, flanked by two armed security
guards.

"But you . . ." Davidson's voice trailed away uncertainly.

"You don't really think I'd let Clyne's crowd keep me
cooped up Inside when the real action was going to be here,
do you?" Torrance said.

Faced by Torrance's rugged professionalism and the impersonal stares of the guards, Michael Davidson felt suddenly weak, as if something inside him had crumpled. He
submitted meekly to captivity.

136

The party halted at an unused repair bay some hundred meters from the control terminus of the underground to make final preparations. Laura and Gerry Clyne stood looking towards the bright unknown at the end of the tunnel, as behind them the men checked their weapons and talked together in hushed voices, speculating on the nature of the action to come.

Laura found herself wondering fearfully just how these hard-bitten veterans of the guerilla war were going to act when the moment of contact came. These men were killing machines, programmed to go into action at the first sight of anything that could reasonably be identified as an enemy. Although they were led directly by Bub Annersley, whom she recognized as holding a fierce loyalty to Gerry, it seemed doubtful to her that anyone would be capable of keeping them in check once fighting began. Many of them must have long nursed thoughts of revenge for comrades who had died, and now they knew the truth that deadly rage must now be directed, not against the guerillas, whom they now knew to have been duped like themselves, but against the as yet unseen puppet masters of the Control Dome. Perhaps, for all she knew, even Gerry Clyne himself harbored such bloody thoughts behind his apparently calm exterior.

She looked into his strong-featured face. "Gerry—let me go on ahead," she said. "It could help."

He looked down at her, a hard light in his eyes. "Help us—or them?" he grated.

"All of us," she said urgently, keeping her voice down to avoid being overheard by the nearby group of men. "You don't really want fighting, killing, if it can be avoided, do you? Most of the people in the Control Dome are just ordinary men and women, taking orders, carrying on from day to day doing a job . . ."

137

"Like the staff at Buchenwald and Auschwitz?"

She paled at the bitterness in his voice, but she went on trying. "Gerry, you know yourself that's not a fair analogy. For God's sake listen to me, please! Many of those people in there are my friends. There's not one I don't at least know by sight, or who doesn't know me. If I go on ahead and talk to them, they'll listen."

"Like your friend Michael Davidson, if he's succeeded in taking over control? Sure, he'll listen to you, and then he'll send a squad in to knock us out—gas maybe, unless he prefers a more final solution—and ship us back where we belong."

"Michael's not like that," she protested. "He's always been against Moule's policy of violence. I thought you understood that."

"Perhaps I understand better than you," Gerry said. "I don't think Davidson is so much against Moule's policy of violence, as against Moule. If he is in control, he will use whatever methods are expedient."

Laura found herself unable to deny the possible truth in what he was saying. His words crystallized some of her own misgivings about Davidson. "All right then, surely that's all the more reason why I should go on into the terminus alone and find out precisely what the present situation is. If Michael has taken over, it's possible that the monitor network is back in commission, but there are no cameras here in the underground, so he can have no idea that you and your men are here. My arrival at the terminus would set off no alarms, and you can wait here in absolute safety until I return." She looked up at him, pleading. "Do you really think I would have done what I have, just in order to lead you into an ambush?"

His expression softened slightly. Placing his hands gently on her shoulders, he said: "No, I don't think that, Laura. But I don't believe we can afford the delay. Surprise is our best weapon, but with every moment that passes, that weapon could be blunted by an increasing preparedness on the part of the people in Control. Having come this far, we have to go ahead now, *all of us*. If we were to do as you suggest, we would be in a negative situation, but once we have taken over the terminus, we shall be able to negotiate from a position of strength. Then perhaps, you can speak for us.''

''All right, Gerry,'' she said, bowing to the inevitable. ''Do it your way.''

He smiled down at her, squeezing her shoulders briefly, then moved away. She watched as he walked from one group of men to another, and found herself taking pleasure in the easy, confident movements of his strong, lithe body. All logic told her it was ridiculous that she should feel this way about a man whom she had known for only a few hours; for a woman of her supposed maturity to fall so deeply in love with this ruthless savage, who would probably end by hurting her badly . . .

Perhaps that was the key to the unexpected depth of their relationship. Since Kurt Jagerman, she had unconsciously picked as lovers men with less drive than herself—weaker personalities whose attractions very soon palled, and whom she was able to discard without pain. Perhaps it was because of the lack of pain that these affairs had also been without the satisfaction she craved. It could be that deep down she was a primitive, with a need to be dominated by the stronger male, to be dragged by the hair . . . She thrust the trend of self-examination aside. If she had learned anything at all from her experience of life, it was that the most certain method of destroying any happiness was to keep reminding oneself of its temporary nature. Everything was temporary, even life itself.

His tour of inspection concluded, he returned to her. ''They're ready. Shall we go?''

Side by side they took their place at the head of the column and began to walk steadily towards the brightness of the Control terminus. Aware of their exposed position, she felt no fear, but a sense of exhaltation that, whatever happened, they were together.

It was only when they emerged at last into the vast underground cavern that her footsteps faltered. Normally the terminus was a center of activity, with vehicles being shuttled back and forth by workers from the Transport Section, but now it was silent, the entire complex devoid of human life, and the vehicles parked in neat rows.

She clenched fingers into damp palms as she realized that the touch of a switch could close the emergency doors, leaving them trapped like wasps in a bottle. If there was someone watching, and a hand poised over the switch . . .

Gerry showed no such hesitation. Under his direction, parties of men separated themselves quickly from the main body and sprinted towards previously allocated key points. Within five minutes the takeover was complete, without a shot being fired, or one human being encountered in the entire complex.

She and Gerry stood together in the deserted office of the Transport Section chief, looking out through the glass wall onto the floor of the terminus below. "I don't understand it," she said. "The terminus is manned at all times by at least a maintenance crew."

Clyne's face was grim. "I can think of several alternatives, but the most likely one is that they knew we were coming, and they're waiting for us up at ground level."

"Then this time you must let me go ahead on my own," she said firmly. "I'll go up in an elevator and call you back on the vid as soon as I've taken a look around."

He frowned, shaking his head. "I don't send women to fight my battles."

"They won't attack me, on my own. I shall be recognized."

"And captured. What good will that do?"

"At the very least, it may save lives," she pointed out, already moving towards the elevator.

"All right," he said. "But if you don't call back within ten minutes, we're coming up."

She nodded. "Ten minutes." The door of the elevator hissed open.

"You'd better take this," he said, thrusting his automatic towards her.

"No, Gerry. I'm with you—but those are still my people up there."

He thrust the gun back into its holster, looking steadily at

140

her. "All right, do it your way. But be careful. I don't want to lose you now."

Clyne watched the door of the elevator close, a sick fear growing in him that this was the last time he would ever see her. He was still deep in this misery when Bub Annersley came into the room. "We found some . . ." The big redhead stopped speaking, a puzzled expression on his ruddy features. "Say, where's the girl?"

"She went up in the elevator to find out what's happening on the surface."

"You sent *her*? But she's . . ."

"I didn't send her—it was *her* idea," Gerry said harshly. "And if you're going to suggest that she may be going to sell us out—don't bother!"

"All right, Gerry. I was just surprised, is all. I came to tell you that we've found some emergency stairs over there at the back of the main repair shop," Annersley said.

"So?"

"Well, I figure they'll be expecting us to use the elevators. Why don't I take a party of twenty men up those stairs?"

Gerry struggled to dismiss his preoccupation with the fate of Laura, and turn his attention to the conversation with Annersley. Certainly it seemed possible that the elevators would be the main focal point of any ambush, with perhaps a token guard on the stairway. He glanced at his watch. Laura had already been gone nearly five minutes.

He looked across to the silent vidphone on the Section Head's desk, then back down at the sweeping red second hand of the watch. He felt a growing conviction that if Laura had been going to call back, she would have done so already. There was no really logical reason for the conviction, it was just an offshoot of the depression that had gripped him since she disappeared in the elevator. In that case . . .

Time . . . did time make any difference, except that, if the situation was bad, with every second that went by it could be getting worse. If Annersley and his men set off now for the surface some forty or fifty meters above, Laura's ten minute deadline would be well past by the time they arrived . . .

"All right, Bub," he said abruptly. "Take your twenty

men, but play it cool. Don't go bursting out like an Apache raiding party. Take it steady, have a quiet look around, and then call me back down here, if you can find a vid.''

''Will do.'' Annersley's round face beamed at the prospect of action, and he hurried away.

Gerry stood for another minute looking down through the inspection window at the hard-faced men who stood alertly at key points around the terminus area, wondering if he had been responsible for walking them into a trap. Then, as if in the hope of kindling some response from the silent vidphone, he went and sat behind the desk. Unwillingly, his eyes moved from the blank screen to the watch on his wrist, to the red second hand which swept round the dial like a tiny, bloody scythe cutting away the links that held him close to Laura, leaving him with the dull certainty that she was not going to call.

It made no difference now whether or not she had deliberately led him into this trap; one way or another, she was lost to him, in the hands of whoever was running the Control Dome now. As she had said, they were her own people up there, and it was unlikely that she would come to any physical harm at their hands. But there was little comfort in that thought. These people could do, *had* done, strange things to the mind of each human being Inside, injecting false memories, erasing old ones, Reprogramming minds completely. He had no doubts about Laura's feelings for himself. Their relationship had been one of those glorious, once-in-a-lifetime pieces of spontaneous emotion—but however deep the roots established by such an emotion, the Programmers were capable of removing them and taking Laura from him forever. Such power, in the hands of human beings, was unthinkable, devilish, open to abuses that were all too obvious.

He knew nothing of Moule, but it seemed likely that the man had been corrupted by this power. As for Davidson, who was obviously unstable in the first place, the prospect was frightening.

The desk vid beeped, and Gerry leaned forward, slamming the switch down with brutal force in his eagerness. But the face on the small screen was not the one he had hoped to see.

"Nothing here, Gerry," said Bub Annersley, "The whole area seems to be deserted."

"Laura?" The name was a knife twisting in his gut.

"No sign of her. Place is like a ghost town. Nobody in any of the offices or apartments within a hundred-meter area from here. You want we should move out further?"

"No, stay where you are," Gerry said, rising to his feet. "I'll bring the rest of the men up in the elevators."

He left the office at a run.

CHAPTER TWENTY-FOUR

Bub Annersley shrugged his barn-door shoulders. "Hell, Gerry, how should I know? Maybe they grabbed her as soon as she walked out of the elevator, or maybe she just decided to take off on her own."

The entire party was grouped in the open square in front of the underground exit. The square was surrounded by single story buildings of uniform gray concrete, with streets of similar buildings leading off at each corner. There seemed no variation in the geometric precision of these streets, as if this were some model town, completely clean of any sign of human habitation, silent, dustless, and dead . . .

Dead, and yet as Gerry stood there he had an overwhelming conviction that his every move was being watched; that someone, somewhere, was playing a cat and mouse game with him. He restrained with difficulty an urge to shout his defiance at the empty, aseptic air.

"We could start a search pattern, using this as the central point," suggested Annersley.

"Looking for what?" Gerry said angrily, resentful of the interruption.

"Well hell, I don't know—people, I guess," Annersley said, frowning. "I mean, where'd they go? Like you said, outside there ain't nothing but Martian desert and damn-all atmosphere. They got to be in here somewhere. Unless . . ."

"Unless what?"

Annersley's red head shook from side to side. "No, that don't make no kind of sense at all," he said. "I was going to say, unless they've gone down into the underground network, using different tunnels to the ones we came through, and now they're Inside."

Gerry released some of his tension in a barking laugh. "Bub, you're developing an imagination. Better watch that." He was about to say something else, when out of the corner of his eye, on the periphery of his vision, he caught a flicker of movement above him. His hand dropped to his gun as something like a shimmering heat haze began to grow swiftly in the air, a couple of meters above his head.

Wrenching the gun from its holster, he fired, the multiple report an enormous affront to the ears in the hitherto quiet street. The haze, still shimmering, but more definite in its bell-shaped form now, began to drop swiftly downwards, to the accompaniment of cries of alarm from the men nearby. There was no time to run, nor, he felt, with a sense of helplessness, would there have been any point in doing so. He had been selected, and he was now being netted as surely as if he had been one particular fish in a small aquarium.

All sound from outside was blotted out as the haze enveloped him in a high-pitched electronic humming that drained away consciousness and will.

He was seated in a chair which supported him in a cradlelike comfort. The man who faced him across the desk was squat and hairless, with pale rounded features that gave the impression of having been moulded out of some grayish plastic. The only touches of color in the drabness of the face were the eyes, which were of a warm amber, almost the same color as those of . . .

"My name is Moule," said the man. "You may have heard of me?"

"The director of the Controlled Environment Project," Gerry said. "Then Davidson didn't succeed."

The amber eyes showed something like humor. "That depends on the viewpoint from which one judges success. Davidson's function in the overall plan was one of catalyst, and he played it to perfection."

"I don't understand. You mean that you knew what he was doing all along?"

Moule raised one grayish hand. "Please, it will only confuse matters if I attempt to give you a piecemeal explanation. Will you be patient, and let me begin at the beginning?"

Gerry shrugged. "I think I have very little alternative. Go ahead."

Moule nodded his approval. "Good! Now, part of the story you already, know, or may think you know, but I want you to try to discard all preconceptions. It has been said that Man is a make-believe animal, never so truly himself as when he is acting a part. In a sense, we all of us play a role, or rather a variety of roles, from the first day that we are born. Sometimes these roles are for our own benefit, sometimes for that of other people. A man in his lifetime can be many people—son, lover, friend, enemy, parent. In each of these he is still himself, but altered in subtle ways according to the part he is playing."

"I don't see . . ."

"Please be patient with me," Moule said. "I enlarge on this subject merely in order to help you understand that what we call 'reality' is, in fact, a subjective abstraction which varies according to viewpoint. As far as you were concerned, until Davidson told you differently, you were quite prepared to believe that Inside—Dome City, as you then knew it—was the only remaining habitable sanctuary on an Earth devastated by atomic warfare. This reality fitted in with the memories that had been programmed into your mind before you were introduced to Inside, and as such you accepted it without question—just as you accepted the conflict situation you found there as a means for channelling off the aggressive tendencies so universally present in your kind."

Gerry found himself staring at the squat, hairless figure with a renewed acuteness. In a speaker so precise, the reference to "your kind" could not possibly have been accidental. Moule must be aware that by the use of such a phrase he was, by implication, placing himself *outside* the human race. If that were indeed the case . . . Gerry forced himself to postpone examination of the flood of possibilities opened up by this supposition, and concentrated on what Moule was saying.

"Alongside this, there was another reality—that of the people in Control, who knew that they were on Mars, and believed themselves to be working on a project organized by the government of Earth for the environmental therapy of criminal psychotics. In a sense, this version is nearer to the truth than the other reality which we have just mentioned; but this too has its flaws, not the least of which is the fact that there is not, nor has there been for the past one hundred and fifty years, any government on Earth."

Gerry became aware that he was trembling. Quietly, without any false drama, Moule was destroying the props that supported his subjective universe. He resisted with difficulty the desire to cringe back into the yielding fabric of the chair, to retire into a state of womblike catatonia in preparation for that final moment when the last prop was removed and he found himself alone in a cosmic emptiness. With a great effort of will, he forced himself to concentrate on the sound of the even voice, and to extract some meaning from the words that flowed over him.

"The missile war is, unfortunately, not just a part of programmed memory. This conflict, begun either accidentally or by design, succeeded in transforming the surface of the planet into a radioactive hell and stripping it of all indigenous life forms. The truly terrible thing about this catastrophe is that it had been foretold so many times in the past by prophets as the inevitable outcome of the scientific 'progress' of a socially immature race. Mankind succeeded in destroying itself, apart from those few pitiful remnants who were either trapped beneath the surface of the planet in deep shelters, or found themselves marooned in the two embryonic colonial projects, one on the Moon and the other on Mars, neither of which was remotely capable of being self-supporting.

"At this point, it was quite clear that unless help was forthcoming from outside within a very short time, the human race in this solar system was doomed to extinction. There were those who said it would be unwise for us to interfere; but others argued that the guilt for the catastrophe lay equally on our own shoulders, because although we had been observing Earth for centuries, we had not intervened earlier when it might have been possible to change the fatal trend. Even some of those who held the latter view were of the opinion that we had waited too long, and that there was now no hope for the survival of Earth-born mankind. But a group, more hopeful, and more sensible of their obligations, finally managed to carry a majority vote against isolationism and indifference, and the remnants of mankind were rescued and transferred to a sanctuary which had been constructed for that purpose here on Mars.

"Even this, by itself, was not enough. Mars could only serve as a temporary home for these people, if they were ever to exist again as free human beings. It is only possible to maintain an intelligent species in an artificial environment for a certain time. Beyond that, such confinement can only result in an irreversible deterioration of the species. Therefore it was essential that a new, more naturally hospitable home should be found for the remnants of Earth's population; a problem of some difficulty, because all the known Earth-type planets in our galaxy were already inhabited by intelligent species in varying degrees of civilization. It was justly argued that there could be no question of introducing Earth humans onto such a planet in the hope that they might live peacefully alongside the original inhabitants. It was quite obvious from our studies of the Earth species that such a situation would only be a breeding ground for yet another disastrous conflict.

"It was decided after a great deal of discussion that the most hopeful solution lay in the cleansing of Earth itself, a vast, but not impossible task with the resources at our disposal, and the experience of some of our members in the terraforming of hitherto inhospitable planets of their own solar systems. Now, after a hundred and fifty years of effort, the project has been completed, and the time has come for your return to Earth. This transfer had already begun, as you may have already guessed from the deserted state of the Control Dome. When it has been completed, those of us here who do not belong to Earth will return to our own systems, and your people will once again be left to their own devices. We shall not intervene again.

"You will not be deprived of your memories of what has happened here. It is felt that such experience may help you to build your new civilization on firmer foundations, without repeating the mistakes of the past. If that is so, then our work here will not have been in vain—if not, then we can only assume that there is some special kind of perversion inherent in the minds of the Earth-type humans which carries with it the seeds of self-destruction. We hope that this may not be so, but only time can give the true answer. One thing is sure, the people of Earth will not be given a fourth chance."

Gerry jerked forward from the womblike grip of the chair. "A *fourth* chance?"

"You must look back into your own mythology for evidence of the last occasion," Moule said. "The legends of gods and giants who walked the Earth, and the stories of lost continents, are not without some foundation."

"And your people saved us then?"

Moule shook his head, a curious expression of sadness on his gray features. "Not us, but another, greater race, in whose footsteps we still totter like hopeful children. They have long since gone from this galaxy, but someday, perhaps, we shall meet them."

"Why am I, in particular, being told all this?" asked Gerry.

"Because your role as leader of the resettled humans will be crucial in these early stages, and it is essential that you should understand fully your responsibility."

"Another role?" Gerry said. "And what if I choose not to play it?"

Moule's heavy features softened. "I don't think we can have been so mistaken in our choice. In any case, a large proportion of the community already look on you as their leader, and will do so with even greater strength in their new environment. It is part of the unchangeable nature of your personality that you will be unable to reject such a responsibility, however arduous. Make no mistake, although Earth has been cleansed and made fit for human habitation again, conditions will not be idyllic. Life will be hard for many years to come. You will be without weapons, or tools, and the only knowledge of technology available to you will be what you carry in your own minds. You will find that this includes a reasonable number of basic skills, but even so the existence of the community will be comparatively primitive for several generations at least, and it may well depend on you alone whether human civilization on Earth is to grow again, or revert back into savagery.''

''You speak of generations, but there have been no births to my knowledge Inside—ever,'' Gerry said.

''For precisely the same reason that only a few months appear to have passed since you first went Inside. This apparent telescoping of memory is a byproduct of the cell-regeneration field which envelops both the Inside and Control Domes.''

Gerry had assumed that he and the others were the descendants of the original remnants of humanity rescued by Moule's people, but now another possibility occurred to him. ''Are we the same people you rescued a hundred and fifty years ago?'' he asked.

Moule nodded. ''The effect of the field is to correct genetic drift, allowing the cells of the human body to regenerate themselves with a hundred per cent efficiency.''

''Rendering us virtually immortal, but sterile?''

''Only whilst you remain within the field,'' Moule explained. ''Back on Earth, the normal aging processes will be resumed, although I think it is fair to assume that a residual effect of the field may result in an increase of at least a third on the natural life expectancy. There will also be less tendency towards debilitating disease, because we have made certain adjustments in the microorganisms necessary to the ecology of the planet.''

''You appear to have thought of everything,'' Gerry said.

"I very much doubt that," Moule replied. "But we have done our best."

"How are we to be taken back to Earth—on this supply ship that Davidson spoke of?"

"The *Orion*?" said Moule. "A myth, created by a few stock shots of a spaceship landing and blasting off, and the occasional presence of two of my colleagues, who played the roles of captain and first officer. We have not used such ships for almost a century, except in the establishment of matter transceiver grids. A receiving station has been established near the coastline of one of the continents in the northern hemisphere of Earth. After you have all gone through, it is keyed to destroy itself. From that point onwards, you will be left completely to your own devices, free of any surveillance."

"You mean that you will be breaking contact with us completely?"

"Our council, in its wisdom, has decreed a quarantine period of a thousand Earth years," Moule said, with evident regret. "It is thought that if the human race on Earth has not finally destroyed itself by that time, then it should be well on the way towards maturity and possible Galactic status. I would give a great deal to know which is to be the true —whether our effort and faith has been, after all, worthwhile. But that is impossible. We shall, all of us, be long dead and forgotten before the results of our work become known."

Although he appreciated Moule's apparent sadness, Gerry found that a kind of exhalation was growing inside him as he began to have fuller appreciation of the task that lay ahead. It seemed to him that this was the kind of challenge which he had been created to accept; nothing less than the responsibility for a world and its entire population. A world which could either slip back into the long night of barbarism, or become the cradle of a new kind of humanity, free of those aberrations that had all but destroyed the race in the past. He would not be entirely alone. There would be others to help him, people whom he already knew from Inside—and then there would be others, who had been in the Control Dome. The first task would be to make sure all of humanity understood that only through unity could the goal be achieved. Laura, Davidson, and Torrance would be invaluable unifying factors, understanding as they did the backgrounds of the hitherto separate communities.

Absorbed in this vision of the future, he was only half-aware that a door behind him had opened.

"Transmission is going according to schedule. The final batch is due through in half an hour."

The sound of the voice shocked Gerry into immediate awareness. He leapt out of the chair, turning to greet the newcomer.

There was something different about her that he was unable to define. She had changed her clothes, and was wearing a silver-gray trouser suit of some iridescent, light material. But the difference was not only in her clothing. There was something . . .

"Laura!" He moved forward, arms outstretched.

She recoiled, avoiding his grasp, and before he could touch her, she had turned and hurried out of the room. He moved to follow her.

"Clyne, please! Don't make her suffer further!" Moule's voice demanded his attention, and as he turned back to face the man he recognized in retrospect the nature of the difference in Laura. Physically she was apparently unchanged, but there was a shadow of pain behind her eyes, a deep suffering that forced recognition. Pain behind her *amber* eyes . . .

"Laura is one of us," Moule said, unnecessarily. "A very courageous and devoted woman."

"But she . . . I . . ." Gerry was incoherent, the prospect of his glorious destiny already crumbling to ashes inside him as he was forced to recognize this new reality. His mind in turmoil, he struggled against an overwhelming sense of betrayal and resentment.

"Please sit down and let me explain?" Moule said.

Fighting the explosive violence that was growing in him, Gerry obeyed.

"It was necessary for the role that Laura had to play that her true memories should be temporarily blocked," explained Moule. "Without such adjustment it would have been impossible for her to assume the identity of an Earth woman with sufficient truth for our purpose. She understood that, and volunteered quite willingly. Unfortunately, there were certain aspects of behavior implied in her programming which did not become apparent until it was too late to intervene."

"You mean you didn't predict what would happen between her and me, is that it?" said Gerry. "And now she's got her memory back, and knows that she's one of the Lords of the Universe, she's disgusted with the idea that she could ever have mated with a rutting primitive," he went on, almost relishing the corrosive bitterness of his words.

"It was . . . unfortunate," Moule said, frowning. "Especially so that she should walk in here like that and come face to face with you. You do understand why it would be completely unwise for you to attempt to see or speak with her again?"

"Do you think I would actually want to, after what you've told me?" Gerry said, trying to ease the searing hurt with a lie. He would get over it in time, he supposed, but for the moment he found it quite impossible to accept the idea that he would never see, never touch, Laura again.

Unfortunate aspect of behavior . . . Was that really a satisfactory definition of the relationship between himself and Laura? And yet there was little doubt in his mind of the truth he had seen in her eyes, the message of pain, which must be the result of the humiliation at facing the sight of the creature with whom she had mated. From her cultural standpoint he could be little more than an animal. And yet he still wanted to be with her, if not as her lover, then as her servant perhaps . . .

No . . . he rejected the hysterical reaction firmly. Gerry Clyne was no woman's slave. Knowing what he now knew, there could be no possibility of *any* relationship between himself and Laura.

"You must understand," Moule said quietly, "that we couldn't possibly have predicted the occurrence of such an emotional accident."

152

"Forget it," Gerry said flatly. "If you have nothing more to tell me, I'd prefer to go now."

"Nothing more, unless there are any particular questions you wish to ask," said Moule. He rose from behind the desk, an elephantine, gross man. His amber eyes burned with a gentle sadness. "Think of us with kindness, and forgive us our mistakes."

Gerry realized that this was an important moment, one in which he should rise above his own petty preoccupations. Swallowing his bitterness, he said: "Thank you, Moule. I shall do my best."

CHAPTER TWENTY-FIVE

He looked upwards, and was reminded of how long it had been since he had seen the stars. It was a warm summer night, and he stood on the sand dune looking towards the arrival point some two kilometers along the coast. For him, there had always been something special about the nearness of the sea, and the gentle murmuring of the nearby surf was another reminder that he was home again.

The others had gathered for the night in a grassy valley further inland. For the time being Bub Annersley was quite capable of doing any routine organizational work that was needed. The real task would begin tomorrow, the exploration of the immediate area, the planning of a more permanent base for this colony of human beings on their own, newly cleansed planet. Davidson was there too, quiet, haunted eyes staring in his pale, cadaverous face, still mentally paralyzed by the revelation of this unguessed-at reality. He would recover and make himself of some use to the community in time. There would be plenty of work for all. After a permanent home had been settled on there would be the task of preserving old skills and developing new ones. And then, later, there would be the children, the forerunners of a new humanity.

Gerry's eyes misted slightly as the chain of association

kindled by this last thought began to lengthen, probing into areas that he would rather not have reexplored. He blinked, and the lights of the matter transceiver grid tower snapped back into focus. For the time being it stood, linked to a transmitter on Mars, and from there with other stations far beyond the solar system and the nearer stars, to the central planets that were the heart of the vast civilization, hundreds of light years away from this obscure, backwater planet, whose people had been given the chance of a new beginning because of the dedication of Moule and a handful of others.

Others like Laura, who was probably already back on her home planet through the magic of this same matter transmission network, back on a planet whose name he could not even begin to guess. There she would live the rest of her life amongst her own people, human beings free of the taint of Earth, capable of living together in peace, and of reaching a height of civilization which, even if he succeeded in his present task, would still, a thousand years from now, be far ahead of anything Earth might produce.

A thousand years . . . His own life could be only a scratch on the surface of such an enormous monolith of time. How could what he did ever have any significant effect on the future?

He thrust the doubts to one side, rebuking himself for his lack of confidence. What he did now, and in the years to come, was—*must be*—important. Moule, at least, had believed that, and it was necessary for he himself to believe it, if he was to fulfill his task. The community needed a firm hand, someone capable of making it grow in the right directions, and equally, someone who had sufficient ruthless devotion to prune off any growth which threatened to develop in the old, twisted directions. Strength, ruthlessness and purpose—all three were necessary to his function, and perhaps it was equally necessary for the execution of such a purpose that he should be alone, dependent on no one . . .

Suddenly, for no apparent reason, he became aware that he was walking towards the grid tower. It was an automatic action which seemed to have no connection with conscious thought, or decision. He had been warned that when the destruct mechanism on the matter transceiver was activated there would be a dangerous release of energy, but the warning had no effect on this strange, involuntary tropism.

The lights of the receiving platform were brightening, the whole installation glowing now, its skeletal outline etched starkly in the darkness. He paused at the brow of a hill, watching as the energy contained in the structure raced towards critical proportions, building swiftly in the visible spectrum. The flaring light seared his watching eyes, and yet he still watched, like a castaway marooned on a desert island staring at the outline of the receding ship; the sight implanting itself deep in his memory, to be recalled time and again over the barren years that lay ahead—a reminder of what might, some time in the distant future, long after his death, be possible again.

The tower shimmered now, emitting coruscating whorls of energy, like a captive sun. This activity was soundless, yet at the same time violent beyond anything he could imagine. Then, abruptly, the pulsing energy began to shrink inwards, imploding down to an intense point of white fire, until at last it was gone, and he stood, feet deep in tumbled sand, overloaded optical faculties plunging him into the velvet dark of blindness. He stood, aware of the murmuring of the surf, and the sound of his own heartbeat, alone . . .

At last the stars faded back into view, but the grid tower was gone forever. He turned slowly. His world, his purpose, lay in the other direction, amongst people of his own kind. He had a duty to them, and to himself, to prove that humanity on Earth could rise again, perhaps this time to find its destiny among the other races of the universe.

And yet he hesitated, aware that something still held him—a memory, a dream . . .

He heard it then, the new sound. A soft movement of footsteps in the sand behind him. He did not dare to turn, only to remain there frozen, facing towards the embryo colony, his mind afraid to interpret what he heard, afraid, yet with the beginnings of an explosion of new hope . . .

He turned, and saw her there, a figure of creamy marble in the moonlight. "Laura!" He moved towards her, and saw that she was smiling.

"I came through just before the destruct order," she said.

"But I don't understand . . . The way you withdrew from me, when we met in Moule's office . . ."

"The shock of that sudden meeting broke down a whole carefully constructed facade of rationalization," she explained. "Until that moment I had been prepared to go back, to accept Moule's assurances that I would forget."

"And now you can never go back."

"No—only forward—*with you*," she said, as he took her in his arms. "Moule understands. He tried to persuade me against it, but finally he realized that this was what I wanted. I shall not be missed there. And a thousand years from now it will make little difference."

One arm round her shoulder, Gerry looked up at the distant stars, and knew that this time the ending of the story would be a different one. When that distant day dawned, mankind would move out towards the stars with hope and love . . .